Early reviews for *Dead Hand*

"*To the Bones*' electric follow up, *Dead Hand*, is a hard-fought battle, from West Virginia to Ireland, for a future free from legacies of pain and plunder. Nieman crafts a richly atmospheric folk horror tale with a thumping heart of environmental justice; like Manly Wade Wellman for a new generation."
— Meagan Lucas, author of *Songbirds and Stray Dogs* and *Here in the Dark*

"*Dead Hand* is riveting, emotionally complex, and beautifully grounded in the landscape and folkloric history of Ireland. I highly recommend it."
— Beth Castrodale, *Small Press Picks*

"Lourana and Darrick are back and, in Val Nieman's hands, you are guaranteed a heart-stopping, white-knuckling ride as she deftly carries the reader from the Appalachians to the Emerald Isle, and beyond. You won't want to put it down!"
— Eryk Pruitt, author of *Something Bad Wrong* and *Blood Red Summer*

Critical response for *To the Bones*

"Nieman does not take her readers gently into the West Virginia night. She plummets us down mine shafts, walks us through grand and terrifying old houses, sends our cars skidding over lonely mountain roads, hides us in dusty attics, makes us watch characters to whom we've become attached melt before our eyes. Hers is a heart-pounding, cinematic, and multi-layered story. It's the sort of rollercoaster ride you race back to the start of the line for, time and again, because despite a queasy stomach and your heart in your throat, you're not ready for the thrill to end."

– Katherine Scott Crawford in *Appalachian Review*

"This nicely paced, suspenseful tale, imbued with detailed knowledge of the Appalachian region and the coal mining industry, is aided by Nieman's rich, artistic language and redolent descriptions of a grim but fascinating literary ecosphere where giant cracks open in the ground, ordinary rock underfoot leaks a kind of vile pus, and orange goo fills the waterways."

– Nicholas Litchfield in *The Colorado Review*

"Part mystery, thriller, and supernatural horror, this tale was extremely enjoyable to read. It's one of my favorite books of the past year . . . At its heart, *To the Bones* is about people trying to survive: economically, personally, spiritually and physically."

– R.B. Payne, *Cemetery Dance*

"Evocative, intelligent prose conjures an anxious mood and strong sense of place while spot-lighting the societal and environmental devastation wrought by the coal mining industry."

– *Kirkus Reviews*

Other works by Valerie Nieman

Novels

To the Bones
In the Lonely Backwater
Blood Clay
Neena Gathering

Poetry

Leopard Lady: A Life in Verse
Hotel Worthy
Wake Wake Wake

Short fiction

Fidelities

DEAD HAND

Valerie Nieman

Avig Press

Copyright © 2024 by Valerie Nieman

All rights reserved. First edition published 2024 by Avig Press.

This is a work of fiction created by the author.
Names, characters, businesses, places, brands, events,
and incidents are either the product of the author's imagination
or used in a fictitious manner. Any resemblance to actual
persons, living or dead, or to actual events,
is purely coincidental.

ISBN: 979-8-218-43504-2

Published by Avig Press
Reidsville, NC 27320

Cover design and author photo by Al Sirois
Book design by Grace Marcus

*For those who go into the dark places,
the deep places,
the lonely places.*

"For he who lives more lives than one
More deaths than one must die."
– *Oscar Wilde*, "The Ballad of Reading Gaol"

The story thus far in *To the Bones* . . .

Disoriented by a near-fatal head wound, auditor Darrick MacBrehon staggers into a sweepstakes parlor at the edge of a bleak West Virginia mining town. But Lourana Taylor, the hard-as-nails operator, doesn't call the cops. She has her own problems with the powers that control Redbird, and this stranger's tale of a police attack and a pit full of skeletons might lead to her missing daughter.

She'll soon have to re-evaluate that decision when they are confronted by his attacker and Darrick mentally pushes back against the man's fear, leaving him warped and dead in the snow. Maybe something inexplicable happened to Darrick down in that mine crack. Or maybe his murky origins are the key to this terrible new ability: A foundling, his name links him to ancient Irish traditions.

His lurching gait and gory head wound launch a panic after he is spotted by locals. Reports of the "zombie" spread, and Darrick becomes the focus of a fading tabloid psychic, the national media, a coalition of ministers preparing for the Rapture, an all-hands hunt for the walking dead — as well as the coal baron Kavanaghs and their legendary ability to "strip a man to the bones."

The buttoned-down bureaucrat faces off against the reclusive family who built their empire by making local authorities into creatures of their will, but he's no longer fighting alone. The unlikely band taking on the Kavanaghs includes Lourana, who's gone ice cold to cope with her husband's addiction and Dreama's disappearance; disgraced deputy Marco DeLucca; and reporter Zadie Person, who is investigating the massive mine acid spill that's turned the river orange. Bodies pile up on both sides, and bonds of friendship and love are tested, until a forgotten mine offers a pathway to the Kavanaghs' inner sanctum.

Chapter 1

Rory Kavanagh stalked through the rooms of Knockaulin House, a place fit to hunt ghosts, if he wasn't already carrying them inside.

First floor, a mirrored ballroom lit by chandeliers imported from France. Glassy marble underfoot reflecting ornate woodwork, and walls hung with genealogical fantasies, ranks of awards presented to his father, grandfather, great-grandfather for their spectacular efficiency in removing coal from the heart of the Appalachian mountains.

Yes, we Kavanaghs have prospered.

Second floor, beds with canopies and windows garbed in heavy brocades. The last light of the sun sparkling through a thousand mullioned panes. Bathrooms frozen in the 1940s, white and slick as ice floes.

Third floor, staff. Well-appointed rooms for the butler and head housekeeper, cramped spaces for the rest. Unused now, all of them gone except for Brodie, who kept the place running with people hired by the hour to cut the grass and launder the sheets. Brodie was generally able to mask his disdain for such a falling-off from the family's grand days.

Rory clattered down the staircases, back to the ground level, as far as he ventured. He did not go into the unpeopled work spaces of the basement. Why would he? And he never ventured into the subbasement, the deep tap root of the house, down in the coal seam.

Down where it began. The harsh presence of his great-great-grandfather.

And nearly ended. His father, rumbling.

Sometimes he heard his uncle, though seldom, his father quashing him as he had throughout his life. Rory would like to know that voice better. The younger brother. Cormac the poet.

Weak, weak chorused the others, and that lash bit into him as well.

He stared out through the leaded glass of massive front doors, frozen shut from disuse, past the iron fence that bounded the property, past the garish lights of cluttered commercial development, to the worn-out hills beyond. His mansion, now. His town, his hills. He'd inherited it three months ago, all of it, the hydra-headed enterprise that was Kavanagh Coal and Limestone. The last thing he wanted.

He doubled back to the library, cheerless without a fire roaring under the great mantelpiece, and thought about calling the butler but decided against it. He'd learned to take care of his own needs at school, and Brodie's precognitive awareness of what Rory might want was intimidating, even scary. He took kindling from the bin, laid up a fire and lit it. It had barely started to catch when Brodie appeared, somehow always just there. The man glanced at the flames without comment.

"What do we have for dinner, Brodie?"

"Dalle Montagne will be delivering, sir. The Tuscan chicken that you favor."

"Thank you, Brodie. You are a marvel."

The old butler inclined his head. Old, yes. Rory realized he did not know how old the man was, only that he had always been there, unchanging, keeping the house, maintaining the family. Rory had been away for most of his life, at boarding school, summer camp, prep school, gap year, and college, but he remembered Brodie just this way even from when he was a little boy, before his mother died. Now the butler turned his hand to tasks below his station, such as cooking breakfast in the cavernous kitchen, which he then plated and served with his usual propriety.

Rory stood close to the small snapping fire, too small for the manorial hearth. He could hear Brodie turning on lamps against the night. The night closing in. He felt hemmed in by more than winter darkness. Back in the family business, against his will, like an Appalachian version of Michael Corleone. His plans would have carried him beyond Wharton and the business degree his father had demanded he take, but which he'd manage to slant away from coal production and toward international banking. Europe, he'd thought. An office in the glittering towers of the Canary Wharf. Maybe Asia, Singapore. Somewhere far from these eviscerated hills and broken people.

Escape, whispered his Uncle Cormac.

But his father's stroke, or so they called it, had summoned him home for what outsiders would have called a deathwatch but which he knew must involve a unique patriarchal blessing: The passage of his father's spirit into Rory's care.

Days passed while Eamon drooled into his pillow. His massive body never moved, but his eyes darted in panic. And then, before his father could pass naturally and take that inheritance with him, Rory had done what was required, placed his hands between his father's, and accepted the legacy of the Kavanaghs.

The memories that came with it were chaotic.

The river running red with acid.

Snow.

An outsider. The sheriff reporting, "There's a man from the government." And then the man was somehow inside the house, inside the crypt room, and with him a woman. They had accosted his father and he'd defended himself, employed that peculiar psychic power that was the Kavanaghs' alone. The woman raised a bone club like a figure from the Stone Age. The room tilted and swam.

Something unknowable had happened.

"You can kill him," said the woman.

The man had refused.

Fool. He gave us time. His father's voice, now always in his mind. *You must find them, you must avenge me.* Others chorused around and behind him, four, five, weaker as the line went further back. He hadn't anticipated the others.

Rory rubbed his forehead, but there was no relief. Must he avenge his father's death? Like in *Hamlet* — "Murther most foul, as in the best it is; But this most foul, strange and unnatural."

In a small, secret place he'd burrowed out within himself, he admitted, If only I'd loved my father as Hamlet did his.

Chapter 2

When her phone went off, Lourana didn't have to look at the number.

It wasn't that she'd bothered setting up unique ringtones. Too much hassle with that. No one called her but Dreama, and Dreama called her every day. More than once a day.

She glanced over at Darrick, who had his work spread out on the hotel room desk, and he looked up with that little crease of irritation beside his mouth, a slight wrinkle between his brows. Lourana stepped out into the courtyard to take the call.

"Hi."

"Momma, how are you?" She always began by checking on her mother, their conversation like it was running on rails, from her first words to the direction the call would take, every time.

Lourana took a deep but silent breath. "I'm fine. Enjoying this nice spring weather. How are things with you?"

Dreama's sigh was not disguised. "Oh, you know."

"Work?"

Silence.

"Are you there?"

"Yes, Momma. I'm not working."

"Did they let you go?" Lourana was angry already, for them to knock someone down when she was trying to fight back to a normal life. The job at the credit union had seemed like a great start.

"I kinda quit. But I think I was going to get fired. I had to take another an afternoon off because I was just, was just . . . "

Lourana could hear sniffling.

"Maybe it's for the best. Sometimes we need a push, right? Why don't you look for a new job, maybe come here to Charleston? You still have friends from school, right?"

Dreama had stayed in Redbird, after all that had happened. She couldn't break free from her grief, as if she was caught in one of those black holes they talk about that pulls everything in, stars, planets, even the light. Lourana was sympathetic, had held Dreama's hand and listened to her for hours, but this misery had gone on far too long. Her daughter had been Cormac's (what — mistress? captive?) for a few months. Not long enough for a deep bond to form. Not like a marriage. As sour as hers had gone, she still had feelings for Steve and always would.

"I can't get over him, Momma. He was everything to me. And then — having him taken — like that." The sniffling progressed to sobs. "At least in Redbird I feel like he's still here, in a way."

Lourana held her tongue. It wasn't as though Dreama could go and recline on his grave like a Victorian heroine: They hadn't yet finished sorting out the bones in the family crypt with the old butler's cooperation and the help of DNA. She watched robins probe for worms, hopping and turning their heads as though they could see them below the ground by using one eye. Or maybe they heard them.

"You know that's just being sentimental. He's dead, and buried now. You're alive and need to move on."

"I wish you were still here."

"Can't do it, sweetie. You know."

"Well, maybe you could come back, for a little while?"

"I do have to finish cleaning out the house," she allowed. "Why don't we make a plan for then? You can help me."

If silence meant that the tears had stopped, and maybe even a little smile had broken out, then Lourana was happy.

"Real soon now, okay?"

"Okay Momma."

"Okay. Love you bunches."

"Love you, too."

Lourana pushed the phone into her jeans pocket and took a mental health break, standing there in the courtyard of the Residence Inn, caught between Dreama and Darrick. She didn't much like it. She loved them both, to the end of the world, but that didn't make it easy to balance their emotional needs.

If she was going to be honest, Lourana had suspected during that horrible time after Dreama's disappearance that eventually she'd find out her daughter was dead, and then, well, she'd go on. That's what you did. She'd been camping out in her life for quite a while. Then Darrick had stumbled into the sweepstakes parlor that night, filthy and broken. When people say "everything changed," then buddy, that was it, in spades. Talk about bonding in a hurry — well, she couldn't criticize Dreama now, could she? But that was different. Life and death.

She heard the trucks gearing down out on the highway, hitting their Jake brakes, because the hill was steeper than maybe you'd expect. A McDonald's sign rose over the interchange. During bad weather, she'd drive there so she could talk with Dreama, get a cup of coffee and sit in the car till her butt was stiff and the coffee long gone. It bothered Darrick to watch her struggling with Dreama over the phone. One night he'd said she was "enabling," and man, she went off like a firecracker. Anyone who'd dealt with addiction the way she had, to say that about her daughter's grief! Well, they'd patched it up and maybe love did get stronger in the broken places, but she tried to avoid taking the calls in the suite where he couldn't get away from the drama.

When she went back inside, Darrick looked up, his eyes somewhat unfocused.

He asked after Dreama and she let him know about the job situation. He was deep into something that looked like official work but could well be more of the mountains of claims and forms to deal with following the theft of his U.S. government car, his disappearance, and the lingering effects of his head injury that provided a convenient cover for the larger problem.

With the Kavanagh situation blown wide open, they'd left Redbird as soon as possible, abandoning her rental house, shifting essentials to this extended-stay hotel in Charleston while they figured out the next step. Darrick found doctors and started treatments, paid for a service to move his belongings from the D.C. apartment into a storage cube. His ability to return to work remotely was a real blessing, because although he seemed stable, they both knew he wasn't ready to think about living and working among crowds of people.

"So what is she going to do?" he asked finally.

No time like the present, she thought.

"I need to finish clearing out the house before the end of the month. I thought Dreama could help me some."

"Help you? Why don't you hire her to do it, and stay here? You don't need to be going back there."

"Just for a couple of days. I don't see as that would be a problem."

Darrick got up from his laptop and began pacing. He looked like her pap, when he was thinking things over, or what he would have called "cogitating."

"Just because Eamon's dead doesn't mean it's safe," he said at last. "The sheriff? All the rest of those people?"

"When you chop off the snake's head, it don't matter if the rest of it's still wiggling around. Kavanagh's creatures got their power from *being* his creatures. I imagine they got enough problems not to be bothering with me."

He came over and enveloped her in a hug. Sometimes Lourana wondered if the chill bumps she got at his touch was entirely love, or maybe a wee little bit of fear as well. Only she knew that other Darrick.

"Please," he said into her hair. "I need you. I can't lose you."

She relaxed into his arms. "We'll drive each other nuts if we don't get a bit of space now and then."

"Why do you want to put yourself back in their sights? You're not helping Dreama. She's spiraling and needs to find her own way out."

"She's my little girl, Darrick. I have to help her."

"You can't help her. Not until she's ready to help herself. Didn't you learn anything from your ex-husband?"

Stung, she said, "That's different."

He said nothing. Didn't need to. She knew Dreama was addicted to her grief as much as Steve had been to Oxy, then heroin.

She pulled away and stood by the sliding glass doors, her arms folded over her chest as she watched the mountains flush back into green. Darrick retreated to the bedroom, as he did when her anger made him flinch. His distancing made her even angrier. *If we can't trust each other . . .*

When he came back out a few minutes later, most of the tension was smoothed from his face. He sat down on the couch and opened the Rand McNally Road Atlas.

"My handy anachronism?" She felt her voice was brittle, harsh.

"It is that. Come on, let's talk about the future, okay?"

So many nights they'd spent considering the possibilities. The Greenbrier Valley. Wheeling. A few other places, because Lourana already let him know she wasn't leaving the Mountain State. Or Dreama.

They were getting close to settling on Harper's Ferry. There were many good reasons: the beauty of the river, the mountain towering above the town, history, an Amtrak connection to Washington.

Most of all, no coal.

The sight of coal stockpiled in a rail yard was enough to send her back to the black room, a crypt carved from the coal for the Kavanagh dead, and a prison for Dreama and her and poor Marco. That terrible Thanksgiving weekend, when a wounded Darrick found his way to her doorstep, and they ended up confronting Eamon Kavanagh at the core of his power.

But we won, Lourana reminded herself. *He tried to suck the life out of us, and Darrick fought back, pushed that evil force right back onto Eamon and left him a dying man. We did it together.*

Chapter 3

This was the purest thing he knew.

Rory crossed the junction and took the trail headed along the river to a long series of waterfalls. The path was springy underfoot, last fall's leaves and dropped pine needles cushioning each stride.

Four miles behind him. He pushed up the pace, breathing deep and regular, the smell of water and earth. A leaning branch of rhododendron whipped him with its spray of pink flowers, leaving a streak of rainwater across his T-shirt. Trail running shoes had replaced cross-country spikes, and painted blazes marked the way rather than flags fluttering across open ground, but the feeling was the same. Whoosh of air into the lungs, the reliable pull and extension of calf muscles and quads and glutes, the occasional jarring footfall on uneven ground. He preferred stream-crossing trails because he'd always reveled in the splash of mud and water, even during icy winter meets.

Cross-country had been the anchor of his life in prep school and college, the only thing that dented the sadness he'd known after his mother's early death. He didn't so much remember her as know what the old photos told him. The few memories had faded as he made few visits home.

You take after your mother, his father rumbled dismissively.

Yes, his mother's brown eyes and fine features. His hair was his father's, but a lighter red. Almost ginger.

Rory plashed through a small creek, ignoring the stepping-stones, and powered up the opposite slope. Making good time, though he wasn't checking.

He'd been more than solid academically, earning admission to Carnegie Mellon without the requirement of legacy, and was good enough in his sport to make the elite Tartans squad. Middling, that's how he thought of himself. The middling man, neither brilliant and elegant like his uncle, nor a massive and intimidating presence like his father and grandfather. He knew them now in a way he not had before, was intimate with their entire lives right through their deaths.

What need has a man for running? His grandfather.

Padraig runs even when he stands still, runs even from his name, his father came in.

I choose to be Rory, he responded.

Simmering silence. Rory, from Ruairí, the Red King. If he chose to use his middle name and not the founder's moniker, then the ghosts would have to accept it.

You are the Kavanagh, whether you will or not.

A roommate once remarked on a letter from home, addressed to Padraig Rory Kavanagh. "Guess you're in trouble. They're using your government name," he said.

For Rory, it was not official but corporate. His male line had become the board of directors to which he answered, a shadow assembly that lived within him, and through him.

I always thought I could keep my hands clean, he thought. Not answering to Padraig had been a start.

"Old Padraig followed the coal under the mountains." That's what his uncle had written in his slender journal of prose poems. Then his son Domnall, the one people called Old Scratch, a hard man whose rapacity spawned the family myth. Then Patrick, in the family's long generations. Then Eamon, his father.

He crossed a rustic bridge that carried the trail to the other side of the river and back to the trailhead. The water came down from the higher peaks, Pineytop Fork of Broad River. Still clean. Relatively.

There were things to be put right. He tried to clear his mind, but it all came pressing back. His father's death. The deliberate destruction of the river by Kavanagh Coal and Limestone, a debt he didn't know how to begin to address. He could not outrun his family or its legacy. He could never outrun himself.

The middling man. He felt more acutely his lack of distinction as he thought of his family. What did he bring to this ghostly assembly? A sense of fair play and sportsmanship? He could hear the laughter.

Chapter 4

Bitty's Luncheonette used to be down near the conveyor belt factory, but when that closed and the Walmart shopping center opened, the owner took a chance and relocated to a narrow storefront between the Shoe Carnival and a discount furniture outlet. Lourana told Dreama she wanted to eat there, and was glad to see the menu hadn't changed.

She was having liver mush on a biscuit, which Dreama called "that black fried stuff," but with a salad instead of tater tots because she knew where calories liked to settle on her. *Just think of it as poor man's paté,* she'd say when her daughter called it repulsive. She wondered if Dreama had ever tasted paté. Probably, living with the Kavanaghs. Then tried not to think about what other tastes she had picked up there.

Now, her daughter sure could use a plate of tater tots. Several, in fact. Lourana watched her avoid eating an egg salad sandwich from which she'd removed the top bread and was picking at the filling with a fork. She'd lost more weight, evident in the hollows around her collarbones and how sharply her cheekbones stood out. She looked a little stretched, a guitar string wound too taut and like to snap.

The clatter of a noon-hour diner filled the space between them. Lourana crunched through a slice of radish. Took a bite out of her biscuit and brushed the greasy crumbs from her lips. Waited until she couldn't stand the silence one second more.

"Thanks for helping out today."

"Sure, Momma. You know I'm happy to help." Dreama offered that lopsided grin she'd shown all her life when she was embarrassed.

"You don't realize how much stuff you accumulate til you have to take it out in boxes."

She nodded.

"Now I don't know where I'll end up, but I'm not getting rid of perfectly good stuff before I know what I need and don't. Always seems like when you throw something away, you need it not a week later."

Pick, pick.

"Those cube things are handy, just shove it all in there and they'll move the whole thing. Not like toting it to a storage unit and unloading it, then having to pull it all back out again. That's how I broke that old china pitcher, moving."

"I guess that happens."

Lourana could barely hear her voice. She was staring down into the wreck of her lunch, hardly had a smile or any reaction at all, except sadness. *Depression, I guess they'd say.* Dreama had always been such a lively, pretty girl, had the best of her daddy in her blue-black hair and dimples. She could turn a fellow's head just like that, but she'd been moping around like a dried-up old widow instead of finding a good man.

That wasn't something Lourana was going to bring up. If her daughter was still hung up on the late Cormac Kavanagh (the name was acid in her thoughts) then her harping wasn't going to change that.

The silence returned.

It hadn't been much different on the drive to Redbird. Darrick had been sunk in his own thoughts, barely glancing her way as he paid attention to the curves on the two-lane road. He didn't like to have music on, or even talk radio, saying it distracted him, so there was just the hum of the tires as the miles went along.

Not that they hadn't had words, and plenty of them, when she'd put her foot down, saying that she was going back and he could come or not as he pleased.

Darrick took her hands in his. He just looked at her for the longest, finally saying, "I can't stand to lose you. You know that." His naked need and fear for her safety made her ashamed of her witchiness. It wasn't about him, though he had plenty to be cautious about all on his own.

We're both of us a couple of stubborn mules, she thought. Guess that's why we're still alive to argue.

In the end, he decided to come. "We're better off together."

"Returning to the scene of the crime," she'd said, trying to lighten things up a bit, but it only seemed to plunge him back into himself and whatever went on in his head.

So they'd departed under a cloud, though it was a bright sunny day. It was oppressive, more than the wordlessness between two people who had long been used to living alone and going about their business without chatter. Most times that was fine, but when there's another person sitting right close for two solid hours, and you're both thinking about some pretty tough times, the quiet hung on your shoulders like a wet sweater.

The waitress came to clear off the table and Lourana snatched the pickle off Dreama's plate before it was carried away.

"Shame to waste food."

"I know, Momma. I remember."

Lourana burned at that comment. She'd been so vigilant when they were having hard times, about food and water and the electric. A memory flashed past, Dreama as a gangly pre-teen, huddled in her winter coat with the heat turned way down in the house, using her fork to distribute watery spaghetti around the plate so it would look like she'd minded her mother and eaten some of it.

The waitress came back with the takeout order and the bill, which wasn't legible but the total seemed right. Lourana figured a 20 percent tip and opened her purse. As she pulled bills from her wallet, she glanced up to see a deputy sheriff looked at her hard. Prichard, she remembered from talking with him once or twice after Dreama's disap-pearance. *Marco always said he was no good.*

"Come on." She dropped the money on the table and headed for the door.

Dreama caught up with her in the parking lot. "What's the matter?"

"The deputy. One of the Kavanagh creatures. He was giving me the stink-eye."

They were almost back to the house when Dreama finally responded.

"That's all in the past, isn't it?"

"I sure hope so. Damned Kavanaghs."

"They weren't all bad." Lourana want to shake her, bring her back to herself, but there was nothing she could say. Or should. Her daughter was still traumatized from seeing her lover destroyed right in front of her.

"I hear that Eamon's son has come back and he's trying to set things right."

Lourana snorted. "Like KCL will do, right? Like building that damn pier that fell in and killed all those people? Like poisoning the river? Like sucking the life out of the town and everyone in it?"

"Maybe he deserves a chance not to be judged because of his father."

Lourana leaned into her window as she got out of Dreama's car at the motel.

"Give *yourself* a chance," she said in her ear. "Leave the Kavanaghs be."

"I love you, Momma." There wasn't much emotion to those familiar words.

Dreama rolled out of the drive with a little wave through the window.

Lourana found Darrick working, having made himself a tempo-rary comfort zone with his laptop and a few file folders.

"Here's lunch."

He looked up, poking his thick glasses higher on his face, and smiled. "What did you bring me?"

"A club sandwich, like you like."

"With potato chips?"

"Uh-huh."

She watched him dive into the white bread and sliced turkey and thought, *You're like Dreama. You just don't know what's good.*

Chapter 5

He couldn't work in the president's office. His father's office.

That's how he still thought of it, because the walls and carpet and the very desk smelled of his father, tasted of him, seemed to retain his image in the shine on antique oak.

Instead, he'd chosen the map room with its display cases of surveying equipment and the big flat drawers with paper maps of topography and geology. Of course, there were computers, too, with big screens where every detail of the Pittsburgh Seam geology could be parsed.

Rory opened a series of encrypted files that showed the inner workings of Kavanagh Coal and Limestone Inc., or what was left following the deliberate dismembering of the company. His father had been executing a controlled retreat from coal into more lucrative fields, had dumped the liabilities and hidden the assets deep in cocoons of shell companies and offshores. The company that would emerge from hiding would be KCL, just the initials, the dusty remains of the industrial past shucked off.

A good plan. Isn't it?

He didn't respond to his father. It was a good plan — he'd known some of it before, the little that had been shared with him, but the scope of this restructuring was both massive and intricate. International finance classes had prepared him well for the new version of the family business, even if his father had claimed to be unhappy with his course of study. He had a disquieting sense that his father had foreseen it all and made plans for him as dispassionately as for the once-beloved mining operations.

In less than an hour, he'd stand before the city council with his own plans.

Rory worked alone. He could summon staff from elsewhere on the sixth floor, but people maintained a respectful space around him, as they had around his father and grandfather in their days. He'd not tested the scope of the legacy that had descended to him, another cursed heirloom he didn't want but couldn't discard.

You will use it. Eamon.

You must. Grandfather.

Darrick murdered me. He will destroy you, if you do not act.

Rory saw the face of this Darrick, black with coal dust from his intrusion through the original Kavanagh mine to reach the crypt room. The terrible intensity of the man's eyes as his father began to draw the life force from his body. Then the inherited memory became confused, his father's body staggered by a blow from the woman, and in the moment of inattention, this Darrick had countered Eamon's psychic force with one of his own. The world had spun and twisted, his father's body hitting the floor, his mind shattered.

He'd raced home to the urgent call from Brodie, his father dying in an ICU suite at Rebecca Kavanagh Memorial Hospital. "You must hurry," he pleaded. "I have a charter jet waiting for you. Time is of the essence."

It had been a very close call. He'd pondered this moment on the flight, the transition he had known was coming someday but which he'd expected would arrive many years in the future and take place in a private and orderly fashion at Knockaulin House, not amid the beeping and flashing of monitors and his father unable to speak around the ventilator tube. Not with evicted doctors and nurses huddled down the hall, waiting to be allowed back to their patient.

Rory thought he had been prepared for the generational shift of ancestral memories and the immense vital force that gave the Kavanaghs long life and the ability to draw on the essential vigor of others, to greater or lesser degree. But his father's mind was disordered and his body broken, so that Rory wondered how this had affected the inheritance. Incomplete, was how it seemed. Not entirely under his control. Like the company. He couldn't undo that damage, or the terrible understanding of just how far his family's power extended. Twisted and fallen, like the pier that had collapsed into the Broad River. At least he could provide some — amelioration — to the survivors of that tragedy.

He added printouts to the briefcase, atop a sleek MacBook Air that held a presentation crafted by the PR department and vetted by legal, and headed out. It was a short walk to the city building, erected on the same solid base of reserved coal as the KCL Building, assured never to collapse into the voids left elsewhere by mining. Birds sang and the air was unusually mild, a balmy March evening. Nothing of desolation or death here, so long as he avoided looking toward the river.

But every step took him past some reminder of the family's hold on the region. The buildings owned outright or secretly through others. Businesses such as favored restaurants propped up to serve the Kavanaghs, or driven into bankruptcy like the department store that had refused to relocate when the land development arm launched a new outlet center by the highway. The dead hand of the Kavanagh enterprise going back 150 years, to the founding of the city and the state itself.

"Mortmain," his contracts professor had said. "Literally, dead hand, from the French. Any time that property is irrevocably transferred to a company or a charitable organization so that the dead are able to control the future through that legacy."

For the Kavanaghs, there was no past. Not really. It was all present, at least for the males. He tried not to think about his mother anymore, because his childhood memories of her were now perversely entangled with his father's. He could see, remember, her hand going up to cover her mouth against a scream when his father had revealed the family secrets.

Rory passed three dispirited protestors carrying signs. "Blood Money!" "Say no!"

They did not speak to him, brave enough to be present but not that bold.

As requested, he was first on the agenda. The fact that the president and CEO of the company would appear in person seemed to have stunned the officials, as the Kavanaghs had been reclusive for decades, working their will through underlings. There had been much interior grumbling about his willingness to appear in public, and his plans to make things right.

We haven't sacrificed so much for you to throw it away on some moral fantasy. Grandfather Patrick.

The dead are dead. Domnall.

I can taste your guilt. Eamon.

He worked through the presentation on efforts to heal the river. There was no argument that the unprecedented and prolonged release of high-potency acid, building on a long history of acid mine drainage, had rotted the supports and brought about the collapse of the recreational pier. The extent to which KCL was liable for a side effect of the mining that supported the entire region was unclear, but the company was being proactive, preparing to assist to the best of its capability.

"While municipal insurance will provide compensation for death and injury, we are concerned with the well-being of the survivors. A fund is being established to provide lifelong care for post-traumatic stress and its effects, and we are announcing construction of a new mental health wing at the hospital."

The council members nodded, some enthusiastically, some grimly. Bitterness and servility, the resentful servant touching the forelock while gritting his teeth. None of them knew the extent of the family's control over the acid, how the spill had been engineered as an escape hatch to shed KCL's coal liabilities and silence opposition against the siting of a high-risk and high-profit biohazards facility.

That was gone now as well, a plan that once brought into the light by a bothersome reporter had burned to ash like a vampire at dawn.

Rory clicked off the presentation. There were no questions.

Tomorrow, he'd again be deep in consultations with KCL lawyers in their ongoing battle with the SEC and EPA and DENR and all the other letter agencies involved in untangling the webwork of shell companies, divestitures, and the rest of the "premeditated fiscal vandalism," as one frustrated official had called it. All intended to shield the Kava-naghs — shield him — from the unveiling of secrets.

Escape, he heard his uncle whisper.

In some ways Rory admired Cormac for having struggled for his own identity and for the love of Dreama. He had refused Eamon's directives and been consumed for his trouble. And now his spirit was condemned to an impotent limbo, forever under his brother's thumb. A ghost to a ghost, and both of them haunting him.

As he started the car (no chauffeur any longer, such trappings soberly reduced), his thoughts turned to the run he'd take in the morning. Those outings offered him an hour or two of release, as he maintained his focus on footing and speed and changes in elevation, his previous times to improve.

When he'd been a cross-country athlete, most of his teams had run as a group, whipping each other on. Now he was at the front, har-ried by his forefathers, unable to hold the middle and conserve his endurance.

He thought longingly about Canary Wharf.

His father's injunction echoed, *You must avenge me.*

Chapter 6

It took her a little while to work up to telling Darrick about seeing Prichard at the restaurant, knowing it would upset him. After he ate, maybe, but then he took a short nap to ease the headache brought on by so much close work, so she busied herself with a walk and visit to the breakfast room, bringing back a coffee for herself, a cup of hot water with a tea bag steeping for him, and a package of cookies from the vending machine.

"How did it go?" he asked, stifling a yawn.

Lourana shook her head. "She's no different now than she was last time we saw her. Except thinner."

"So you couldn't talk her into relocating?"

"Not to Charleston, not to wherever we end up, not to Miami blessed Beach. That girl is the stubbornest thing."

Darrick looked at her and didn't have to say a word.

"Ahh — one other thing. I saw somebody at the diner. That deputy, Prichard."

"Did he see you?"

"Yes." She took a sip of coffee.

"And?"

"He kinda gave me the stink-eye."

Darrick was up and pacing, agitated at the news. "I knew this was a terrible idea. We should never have come back here."

"We gotta finish up with the house."

"I already said what we could have done." He peered out the glass doors as though expecting to see a SWAT team headed their way.

"So, what will they do?"

"Who knows what they'll do!" He was almost shouting, now, his face flushed. "You know how they operate. We'll probably end up dead in a ravine or at the bottom of the river. Or worse."

"Honey, I don't think it's like that anymore." She wasn't going to let on how shaken she was, because one of them had to keep things on the level, and it appeared it wasn't going to be him. "We'll turn in the keys and be done here, forever. Promise."

"Until Dreama calls you crying."

"Not even then."

He began packing up his office materials. "We'll get ready now, get everything done, so that tomorrow we can be on the road after we turn in the keys and get the deposit. When is that again?"

"10 a.m. at the property manager. Third floor of the McNulty Building. I think you're overreacting."

"I think I'm reacting just fine. They know we're here — how long will it take them to find us? How many hotels are there in Carbon County?"

Lourana could feel an argument building that she had no desire to pursue, because he was right. When she'd seen the deputy's face, she knew. *It's not over.*

She followed his lead and began packing her suitcase, leaving out just what she needed for morning. Not that they'd brought much.

They drove to the little house that Lourana used to rent, up on the hill above the Walmart. It looked shabby in the clear spring light. As they entered, Darrick stumbled on the step, confirming what she thought she recognized back at the hotel. Emotional stress still caused his ataxia to re-emerge, even with medication.

It took only minutes. She and Dreama had already cleaned. She did a final check of the closets and basement and he carried the last three boxes to the car and stowed them in the trunk, heirloom dishes and things like photo albums that she'd not carried away before but had not wanted to put in the storage cube.

At the door, she looked around before shutting off the overhead light. Darrick was waiting and he offered his hand.

I always expected to leave here, with Dreama or without. I couldn't have imagined things would have ended up this way.

Chapter 7

The sheriff had gotten the report from Prichard and come hat in hand, literally, his black straw sheriff's hat clutched in his meaty paws, to deliver the news.

"He didn't have no doubts about it, sir. It was Lourana Taylor. She was having lunch with her daughter."

Dreama. His uncle summoned the image of the dark-haired young woman he'd loved. *"And all that's best of dark and bright / Meet in her aspect and her eyes."*

Rory tried to focus. "Just the two of them?"

"That's right."

Rory could feel the sheriff evaluating him. Comparing him with his father, and not in his favor. He maintained a calm, smooth exterior, but inside was a clamor of Eamon and Padraig urging immediate action.

"Do you know if Darrick is with her? Where they might be?"

"We started with the house she used to rent, but it's empty, so then we started checking the hotels and B&Bs and such. Finally tracked them down, and it's the two of them, yes sir, at the Holiday Inn on the other side of the lake. But they checked out around 5 am."

"They're gone, then?" Rory hoped, in his secret self, that they'd slipped away.

"Not quite, sir. The rental company said she's gonna come in later this morning to claim her deposit and turn in the keys."

Eamon's awareness pushed forward. *That's our opportunity.*

Rory could not hide his distaste. How much of a threat was she, really?

A memory appeared from the distant past. Domnall's past. Strike-breakers evicted from company houses had set up a camp in the bottom down by the tracks. He saw the rail car fitted with World War I surplus machine guns. How the bullets tore through the tents. Women and children, their fathers walking the picket for the United Mine Workers. Ragged. Cold. Hungry. And then bleeding in the snow.

The Pinkertons took care of that problem, root and branch. His great-grandfather, called Old Scratch for the devil he was to the miners. *We'd have killed Mother Jones, too, could we have caught her.*

Lourana, growled Eamon, reclaiming center stage. *If we have her, then Darrick will come.*

And his forefathers chorused, *We're not ready for Darrick. Not yet. We need to repair the damage.*

Rory had been aware how closely the sheriff was watching him, wondering if he was losing the battle to keep this internal debate from showing on his face. He controlled himself and got the details from the sheriff, the name of the rental company, the time of the appointment.

So he found himself behind the shabby desk at the property management office, in a business and a building that KCL owned (though few people knew that), waiting for Lourana and Darrick.

For all the distortions in his father's memory, Rory recognized her immediately. She wasn't wearing a silly sweatshirt this time, but a flowered blouse and slacks in shades of melon that had probably come from Walmart.

His father seethed, remembering how her sneak attack had left him vulnerable to Darrick. Just for a moment, but enough. *Where is he?*

"Thank you for being on time," Rory said.

"I'm on a bit of a deadline myself." She smiled. "So where do I sign?"

"Here, and here. We've already had a look at the house and everything appears to be in order."

She took the pen he handed her, leaned over the paper and signed, her signature carefully legible.

"And where are you headed, Ms. Taylor?"

"I don't altogether know," she said. "Thinking about the Eastern Panhandle, but it's still all up in the air."

She stood and set a ring with three keys on the desk. Already she was turning toward the door.

"Are you going to miss Redbird?"

As she glanced back, he saw something like regret in her eyes. His father remembered how she had always been impervious, her emotions locked down tight. Not any more.

"Not really."

"No sentimental ties, then? I understand," he said. "Still, you can never entirely leave a place. As it happens, I believe you knew my father."

"You do look kinda familiar," she said affably, letting her hand fall away from the doorknob.

"My name is Rory." He could feel his father's presence rise within him, unstoppable, felt him in his throat. "But you knew me as Eamon Kavanagh."

As his voice deepened and roughened, he watched her face tighten into a mask of terror.

He couldn't say for sure who it was that controlled his movements, but he caught her by the arm as she tried to get the door open. There was a riot in his head, his father primary but Cormac struggling to emerge, while Padraig and Domnall lent their strength to Eamon's ascendancy.

Most women would have screamed, but Lourana just stared, frozen at the sight of him.

Rory gained some control over his voice, at least, though he could hear how each word revealed the strain to do so. "We won't harm you if you bring — him."

Eamon, wild as a wounded bear, could not allow that hated name.

Stop holding back. Old Scratch, vindictive as his grandson Eamon.

Take her. Take her now. Eamon reached out through him. Rory felt his own will slipping away, as though he, too, were being plundered of his life force by his father. He could see the lines of connection form-ing, a golden shimmer binding her to him. To them.

But then Cormac found a way to intervene, his presence unex-pectedly strong. Steel, concealed by silk. His presence gave Rory enough power to dampen the attack.

Lourana gulped air like a drowning person rising one last time before going down.

Still, she would succumb. Just more slowly. Painfully. She would do as they demanded. Rory was revolted by the memories his fathers fed to him, the corrosive touch of their spirits on his thoughts.

He was shocked back to the world by the sound of the door han-dle turning, the creak of hinges, and a voice — "What are you doing? I thought this would be quick."

Darrick came in, and now Rory felt that sense of being frozen, as the tumult within reorganized around one presence.

They knew each other at a glance, Eamon and Darrick, and between them, like civilians caught between the lines, Rory and Lourana.

Darrick exerted that psychic force, one that Rory had expe-rienced only through Eamon's memory, and the last of the binding on Lourana snapped. She slumped toward the chair but with a final intense push, Darrick halted the Kavanaghs, pulled her upright and out the door, and they were gone.

Rory hung onto the edge of the desk as he found his way back to his seat. He felt as if he'd been squeezed in a vise, the jaws on one side no less implacable that those on the other.

I'm not my own man, he thought.

Chapter 8

She kept thinking about that Tom Petty song, the one about not having to live like a refugee. That was exactly how they were living, now, on the road and on the run. It wasn't anything you'd want to sing about.

They'd fled Redbird like a pair of scalded cats, taking out as much cash from the ATMs as they could get and topping up at busy places they were passing through. Lourana thought that maybe all those nights she spent watching true crime TV was useful now. Skills.

They hopscotched around Virginia and Maryland, a couple of nights here, a couple there, at B&Bs and faded local motels where people were happy to take crisp $20 bills and didn't have to enter computer reports.

A hard glance by a man on the street in Fredericksburg, MD, sent them flying to a small hotel on the fringes of Breezewood, PA, a wasteland of truck stops where semis roared down the interstates all night and everyone in the Waffle House was a stranger.

A spam call with a 304 code had them turning in her phone at a Verizon store and buying a burner.

And so it went. They were effectively homeless.

There had been a lot of silences those first few days. As they sat outside an Arby's eating lunch, Lourana got the giggles.

"What's wrong?" asked Darrick.

"Nothing. Just — oh, it's silly."

He cocked his head and watched her, that birdlike motion sending her off again into stifled laughter.

"It's just — it's just — I started thinking about Rory, and what he looked like, completely out of control. I expected his head to start turning around like in *The Exorcist.*"

"Pretty accurate, really."

"Because they're inside him, right? All of them?"

"I don't know how many 'thems' there might be."

"What did that feel like?"

Darrick pushed a drop of barbecue sauce around the wrapping in his lap. "I can't really explain it. There's a group, five of them as far as I can tell, and each one seems to be pushing for attention or access to Rory's mind and body. I keep thinking about the line, 'My name is Legion, for we are many.'"

Lourana figured that was from some old philosopher, or the Bible, but she wasn't going to ask.

"I can identify Eamon right away, his rage, and how he's only somewhat coherent," he added, "and Cormac, too, maybe because I actually knew them, or they're more recent. The others are in the background. Less defined. But there's a dark thread through them all, a similarity."

She could hear Eamon's harsh, mocking voice from their encounter last year, when he had explained to her how the Kavanaghs inherited more than massive wealth and a creepy old mansion, how as the patriarch of each generation approached his death, he'd pass along the memories and powers he himself had gained from his ancestors, as well as his own spirit and life force. Like Dreama once told her, we don't eat the rich, the rich eat each other.

"And no one else — feels like that?"

He shook his head. "No. Not so far, anyway."

Lourana was sorry she'd brought that up. Darrick was troubled by the memory of the men he'd killed back in Redbird—in self-defense, true, and because he hadn't understood what his new power was, emerging after he'd been battered nearly to death in a case of mistaken identity and thrown down into a mine crack. It took him a while to understand what it was, his deadly response to strong emotion that turned out to be a weapon against the life-sucking Kavanaghs.

"So what's Rory, how is he, in all this?"

"He's pretty low-key, drowned out by Eamon. Almost like he wasn't there, just his body being moved around by the others. Now I understand how they used to talk about people being possessed by demons."

"Possession is nine-tenths of the law," Lourana said with a little grin.

"Actually, the phrase is 'possession is eleven points in the law, and they say they are but twelve.' "

"Picky picky. Where did that come from?"

"From your home turf, actually. It's Scottish or Irish or something, originally, but it came up during the Hatfields and McCoys feud."

"I don't think they were talking about the same thing at all."

That conversation seemed to break the silence between them, unclenched some of the fear, and they talked out everything about the Kavanaghs until the pressure was relieved, until it didn't knot her stomach so her muscles were sore. It felt like she was clinging to a plank of wood in a shark-filled ocean, and Darrick likely felt the same. Adrift and imperiled by things they couldn't see. Or maybe that was paranoia.

"Do you think . . ." she began.

"What?"

"Do you think that maybe that was it, the thing with Rory? One time? Just because we were there in Carbon County and Eamon couldn't pass up the opportunity to get revenge?"

His face showed that he was considering that possibility with a kind of insight that she didn't have.

"No. We know now that they've still got their creatures watching out for us. And when I encountered Eamon at the office — he's beyond any shred of rationality, and he is in charge. Definitely the CEO of this enterprise. His son is just something to be used, and he'll drive him to find us again."

"That poor kid."

"Remember, he's a Kavanagh. He must have known about this, what would happen."

"I know, but still. To have something like Eamon rampaging around inside your head." It made her skin crawl again, and she rubbed her arms again the chill bumps.

They balled up the remains of their meal, the French fries and roast beef less tasty now that they'd chewed on their predicament. Lourana took the bag to the trash on her way to the rest room.

She looked at herself in the mirror, harsh fluorescent lights making her look greenish and haggard and 20 years older. She pulled the elastic out of her ponytail and ran her fingers through her hair, then fastened it back again. This life on the run was no good. They'd been wandering with no direction, traveling in a sort of limbo, far from Carbon County but not any closer to Darrick's home in DC. God knows where they'd sleep tonight. Any thoughts of finding refuge in the historic towns of the Eastern Panhandle were gone, since she'd so innocently mentioned it to Rory. She splashed some water on her face, pinched her cheeks, and headed back to the car.

As she was buckling her seat belt, Darrick said something that brought her up short.

"I'm worried about the car."

"Why's that? It's running fine." She loved the tough little old Subaru wagon that had seen her through snow and ice, bad roads and no roads.

"It has a license plate. Registration. When we went through that toll booth yesterday, I started thinking about how we could be traced with that, even if we're using cash and doing all the other things."

And the Kavanaghs have direct access to law enforcement, she thought.

"Maybe we should get out of the country. Go to Canada or something."

"For good?"

He shrugged.

Easy for him to say. He had no one to tie him here. Of course, all she had was Dreama.

She'd continued to talk with her every day, keeping it vague about where they were. "Just vacationing." Dreama was so involved in her grief that she never questioned why her stay-at-home mother was gallivanting all over creation with this guy. Lourana had not told her about Rory and the attack at the property manager's office, not wanting to worry her with a problem that didn't involve her, not directly at least. But she'd warned her, in a way.

"Honey, I think you really need to get out of Redbird."

"Momma . . ."

"I know. You'll tell me you aren't ready." Lourana couldn't think of a reason she hadn't already used, trying to convince her daughter.

"It's not like I have someplace I want to go."

"Maybe you're just not thinking big enough, sweetheart. You have your whole life in front of you. You could go to New York or L.A. and start all over again."

"I didn't leave a thing in those places that I need to go back after," she said, and Lourana heard an echo of her pap, and herself, in that phrase.

"Well, anyway. Stay clear of the Kavanaghs, at least."

"I will. Cormac, you know, he wasn't like the others. And I miss him so much." Lourana didn't have to have Facetime to know about the tears in her eyes. "But Momma, you be careful, too. Darrick is not exactly a normal person either. You don't know him all that well, who he really is."

And that was true enough, she thought as she came back to herself and realized he had been waiting for a response, his gray eyes sort of unfocused behind those thick lenses.

"Sorry. Wool-gathering." She rummaged around in her purse for a couple of mints and gave him one. He turned his attention back to the road, which was a narrow, twisting two-lane, just a few cars, though occasionally they'd meet a Dollar General truck barreling along from one barely functional crossroads community to the next.

She kept seeing that scene in the office, Rory such a placid, pleasant young man until Eamon emerged. She'd been terrified to re-encounter an enemy they'd thought was dead and gone, the end of the nightmare. Maybe it shouldn't have been a surprise, since Eamon had so harshly demonstrated how he'd taken over his brother and father, but that Rory would have willingly carried on this tradition — well, as Darrick said, he'd been raised to it, like the undertaker's kid. They'd vanquished the monster only to have it roar back to life — what would have happened if Darrick hadn't been impatient and opened that door? The humor in the weirdness of it all was just whistling past the graveyard.

And Darrick, that was another matter.

He had seemed so hapless at first, when he'd staggered into her sweepstakes parlor with a wild story about being dumped down a mine crack and crawling through skeletons to get out. It had been enough to make her hide him, help him, in hopes he had information that would lead her to Dreama. Her daughter was dead, she had been sure after so long a time, but maybe, maybe alive. She had to hold onto that hope. Rory's transformation just brought back memories of how Darrick also had turned out to be — something else. Able to kill people just by pushing back their own hatred, fear, anger. That security cop sliding dead to the snow-covered pavement.

"In 500 feet, turn left."

The GPS was a good companion on these backroads. Mostly she ignored it, sitting in the passenger seat of her own car because Darrick had to drive, he was such a control freak.

She needed to figure out this Darrick thing.

He'd barged into her life and taken her down rabbit-holes she could never have expected. While she'd studied on the Kavanaghs a long time, unable to hold them accountable for their crimes, he came in and took them on directly. He'd been willing to put himself in their path, protecting her, and the love that had blossomed so quickly as they were forced together in danger had not gone away, though it had changed.

His ability to counter the Kavanaghs had been providential, that was true, but there was no explanation of where his psychic power came from, if that could change or even evaporate as quickly as it had arrived. Just because he'd been the good guy, would he always stay the good guy?

How did you give your complete love to a man like that? She had loved Steve, in that way you do when you're young and stupid. His descent into addiction had made her an accessory — she helped him because that's what you did for a husband, until she finally decided she wanted to live more than she wanted to let him keep sticking needles in his veins. There was a hunger inside an addict, something that could not be appeased. Darrick wasn't like that. He was kind, considerate, passionate, but a chunk of who he was now could not be reached. At least by her. Love is blind? It could look the other way from addiction, and maybe from this dangerous psychic ability. Or maybe not.

"You have arrived," said the GPS.

This little town on the edge of a national forest had seemed like a good destination for the night as they looked over maps of the area. They pulled up in front of a genteel Victorian with oversized shrubs but a welcoming look for all that. A "Vacancy" sign swung below a basket of purple flowers. The couple who said they'd bought this place last year in hopes of attracting hikers and skiers seemed overjoyed to have guests, and it appeared they were the only ones.

"We'll put you in the Garden Room," said Rick, who wore a rainbow pin in case there was any doubt. "It has a door onto the side courtyard."

"Private," added Abdul.

The room was comfortable, with period furniture including a washstand and chamber pot filled with flowers, along with a private bath. The courtyard was small and dense with greenery.

They got advice on where to eat (really just one place) and took it, getting a good meal of pot roast and homemade bread. Full and tired, they returned to the room and stretched out to watch television.

Prime and Netflix were available, and the stream from Spectrum. Hard to believe that with so many shows, you could run out, but the limited intersection of their tastes narrowed the menu. He liked serious shows, TCM stuff, while she was happy with old comedy series and *Jurassic Park*.

Finally, they came across a documentary about Ireland. Aerial shots showed soaring cliffs, sheep spilling like milk down a green hillside, ruined castles, all set to the lilting sound of harps and pipes and a chorus of women's voices singing in Gaelic.

"Clichés," he scoffed. Still, he continued to watch intently. Ireland was all that Darrick had as an anchor in the world, a foundling whose DNA search had drawn a tight circle on the island but failed to unfurl a single leaf on his Ancestry tree. His history began and ended with an orphanage in New York State, and some obscure comments by the priest who had found him and the nurse who'd protected him.

"We should go there," she said, surprising herself. "To Ireland."

"Really?" He looked at her like she'd turned blue or something.

"You could find your roots, maybe. You said that your genetics are all Irish, so where else would you go?"

"Nice idea, but since I don't have information on my father or mother, I can't trace my roots. No parish records or Ellis Island logs for me." There was a hint of self-pity in his voice, but Lourana couldn't fault him. She knew exactly who her people were, and exactly where the most of them were buried up on Whitestone Run.

"Even so, you could at least see the place," she pressed. "And it's not like we have anywhere special to be."

The show had shifted from scenery to history, the Famine and the coffin ships. Emaciated women found dead at the doors of the workhouses.

"We'd be away from here, anyway." He stared at the screen, then asked, "Do you have a passport?"

"No. I never needed one."

"Just like most Americans."

His dismissive tone fired her up. "And I'm sure you do."

"Yes. But I've never used it," he admitted. "Always kept it current, but I never went anywhere."

She had thought about traveling, though the lack of time off from work or money to go stopped her from ever doing more than dreaming. Driving across the country was one of those things you talked about but never did; taking a trip overseas never made it to the talking stage. Her family used to go every year to Myrtle Beach, like most everyone in West Virginia, so she could say she'd seen the ocean.

"So where do I get one?"

"We'll need your birth certificate."

"I keep hold of that."

"And a photo. The application can be made at post offices and courthouses. Expedited, it would take a few weeks, unless it's a life-or-death situation."

He gave her a look and she gave him one right back. It might could be life or death, but not a soul would believe the story.

Chapter 9

He was just another young professional, an insurance broker or banker, taking a short respite from a hectic schedule to grab a mid-morning coffee. Or at least to casual bystanders, though people at The Black Diamond Roastery were anything but.

As he waited to order an Americano, Rory could feel their attention — mostly covert glances, but a couple of open stares. Everyone in Redbird knew who he was. "The young heir." Almost, he admitted, the Young Laird of some feudal domain. Everyone knew the story, or at least the story as it was printed in the paper and blared on TV. The distressed KCL empire. The bones in the basement.

He'd come in behind Dreama, who was ordering a decaf latte with soy milk. She had not seen him join the line two spaces behind her, but when she turned to the pickup area, her eyes caught his.

Dreama. Cormac's emotion suffused Rory's thoughts.

"Hello," he said, struggling to keep Cormac out of his voice.

"Hi." She glanced away, saw the barista set her cup on the counter. "That's mine."

She collected it, stuffed a dollar in the tip jar and threaded through the line to a place near the window. Rory took his and started for the door, but found himself detouring to her table.

"Might I join you?"

She nodded slowly. Reluctantly.

They sat and sipped in a bubble of their own silence, while around them people chattered and stared, it still being a novelty for one of the infamous Kavanaghs to appear on the streets of Redbird.

Coffee grinders and foamers buzzed intermittently, and Kenny G filled in the gaps.

"I'm Rory Kavanagh. We've not officially met."

"Dreama Taylor." She appraised him over the rim of her cup. "But we have met, in a way. Through Cormac. Am I right?"

He felt himself blush as NSFW memories filled his mind. "You understand my — unique situation. And I think I can understand how you feel, but please know I am trying to make things right. For the town. For you."

Don't let her get away.

Rory pushed his uncle aside. "I would like to be able to talk with you — less publicly."

Her eyes widened.

"At a restaurant," he hurried. "Would you agree to meet me for dinner? Just so that we can talk without all this attention. Wherever you would like."

She put down her cup, pushed back in her chair, stood. He felt Cormac's panic rise.

But she didn't walk away. After a moment, she said, "Okay. How about The Reef?"

Cormac shared that was where they had dinner, their first and only public dinner, a couple of nights after Christmas when he'd presented her with a replacement for her broken necklace.

"That would be lovely."

The dining room was suffused with dim, turquoise light spilling from the fish tanks that lined three walls. Shadows flickered as specimens from clown fish to sharks to frowning groupers finned through coral landscapes. The food was adequate — everyone said the owner only operated the kitchen to underwrite his passionate love of tropical fish. Electric candles set in conch shells lighted the small tables, which were all empty. Only part of the reason was the lateness of the hour.

Rory and Dreama barely spoke through the salad course. Rory was occupied with quelling his forefathers, while Dreama seemed to be lost in sad memories. They each contended with secrets, but it was an unequal contest, as she knew only a little about the Kavanagh clan while Rory knew everything that had transpired between her and Cormac, could feel the weight of her breasts in his hands, and he burned with Cormac's desire. He focused on the fish. After a few uncomfortable minutes, he was able to proceed with dinner and conversation.

"First, thank you for agreeing to join me tonight. It's a great pleasure for me," he said, while giving the nod to the owner to leave another bottle of wine and disappear. "As I said, I would like to make amends for my family's actions. You and your mother were the worst affected."

"Other than the ones on the pier."

"Yes. And I've been working to address that, along with the damage to the river. It was a horrible series of events."

"But you were not involved."

"No, I was far away, and not yet involved in the business."

For good reason, Eamon added.

"Cormac was not at fault either." She cut into her filet with a little more force than one would expect, from hunger or anger, he wasn't sure. "He suffered because of Eamon. We all suffered."

He broke open a roll, broke it again, carefully buttered one quarter and then another. The more attention he paid to the moment, the more precise his actions, the less the others were able to push forward. Be here now, he reminded himself, be here now.

"You know people thought I was being held captive."

"Yes."

"It wasn't like that."

But it certainly must have looked like that, Rory thought.

We had to protect ourselves, Eamon responded.

Cormac brought her into the family without consulting us. His grandfather.

I love her. I wanted to keep her close. Safe. All we wanted was a life together. Cormac.

You know how it's to be handled. Marriage. Eamon.

I was never the Kavanagh.

Nor could you ever be. From the depths, Domnall backhanded Cormac with that remark, delivered with disdain.

Rory knew he'd been silent too long.

"I know that Eamon consumed Cormac's life. I saw it happen." She looked at him, direct, unflinching. "But then Cormac was still *there*, inside his brother. Did you, did Eamon . . . what I'm asking is, are you carrying on the family tradition?"

Rory couldn't look at her, allow her to see what was going on inside him. He kept his head down and stared at his hands, tried to focus, as Eamon was pushing to speak and so was Cormac.

I thought I could manage this.

He pushed back from the table, his napkin sliding to the floor as he turned away.

"Rory?" Dreama's voice cut through the tumult. Then, in an entirely different tone, "Cormac?"

Cormac was filling his mind, his body. He became a bystander as Cormac moved to her side and knelt to take her hand.

"Dreama. Oh, I've missed you."

It was his voice and Cormac's blended, as his body felt like Cormac's, two beings slightly out of phase, awareness rippling across the gap.

"I've missed you, too." Her hand tightened on his. "I didn't think I'd be able to go on living without you."

Rory felt a shudder, the eeriness of being two and one.

Their heads came closer together. *A spark of light on her hair, an evening star appearing in the night.* Rory could taste his uncle's poetry, as he could almost taste her lips.

She opened her mouth and and he, they, leaned closer. When they kissed, the intensity of the contact was beyond physical, was spiritual, was lifting him out of his body. He could have flown away in that moment and left the shell to the sparring fathers.

It was Dreama who broke off, pulling away with a little sigh. She dabbed at her eyes with the napkin, then compressed her lips.

"Thank you."

He inclined his head, unable yet to speak.

"It makes me think of this old movie, the one where Patrick Swayze is a ghost. I can't touch him but I know he's there, he's in your touch and your kiss. And when you speak, it's him, or almost him."

Not only him. Eamon shouldered his way forward. *Say it.*

"Not only him." His father's harshness made her shrink away, and Rory pushed him back. "Also Eamon, and my grandfather," he creaked. "That's how it is, to live with this. Inheritance is not all it's cracked up to be."

Dreama hadn't fled, as he thought she might, but then in asking for Cormac, she must have known that the others would have access as well.

"I am my father's son, I can't help that, but I am not like him." Rory rested his closed fist on the table. "I will not allow him to rule me." He could hear Eamon's sarcastic laughter. And feel Cormac's need.

Chapter 10

Well, that was awkward.

They'd stumbled off the overnight flight into a gray morning and a problem.

"I'm sorry, sir, but there's a bit of a hiccup with your car," said the clerk at the Hertz counter.

"Excuse me?"

"Um, we had a car go into the shop, and that leaves us short. Simply no automatics available. Would you be wanting a manual then?" He gave them a bright smile, then looked down and typed a bit on the keyboard. "Sir?"

Darrick was just standing there, not responding. Lourana stepped forward.

"If that's what you have, then I guess so," she said, glancing over at Darrick again.

"I can't drive a stick," he blurted out.

"Ah." The clerk seemed to add *just like an American* without saying a word.

"Well, I can. Maybe we could exchange it later?"

More typing. She watched the rain stream down the windows of the terminal.

"We'll have the model you requested in two days. If you're staying in Dublin, you scarce need a car. We have the DART system, that's the train, and excellent buses," he said, quietly, again with the implicit comment. "You can take a bus to the city center from three Euros 30, or a shuttle for 7."

Seemed like it was that or cancel, and she knew there was a heavy penalty for the cheap rate they'd pre-booked. And they *were* staying in Dublin, though for how long she didn't know.

"Darrick? Okay?"

He nodded stiffly. *Was it just the tranquilizers or was something else going on with him? Shouldn't the pills be about worn off by now?*

"We'll get that sorted, then. Céad míle fáilte — welcome to Ireland, if I failed to say that earlier."

"Thank you. Could you perhaps cover a taxi, as you can't provide us with a car?"

More typing, and done.

Lourana steered Darrick toward baggage claim. By the time they had their luggage, he'd come out of his funk and took charge of finding the Uber location and the promised ride. She was relieved, all around, as she didn't need to be driving a strange car on the wrong side of the road right now.

They'd worn themselves out with running, waiting on her passport to arrive. His back-door contacts at State had pushed through the application at almost a life-or-death pace. They booked a last-minute flight out of Philadelphia, leaving her car in a long-term lot far off the airport property.

It wasn't til they got off the shuttle at the terminal that Lourana was able to admit she'd never been on a plane, much less one that was flying across nothing but water. Darrick offered her one of his pills, but she knew from hard experience that was a road she'd best not go down. He'd managed the trip so far with medication and avoiding crowds — they retreated to the chapel at the airport, unused throughout their wait — and booked first-class seats to insulate him from the discomfort of someone's foul mood.

As they took off, he talked her through the process. The clunk of the wheels retracting. Normal. The whine of the flaps. Normal. The stomach-dropping dip when they reached cruising altitude. Normal.

Once they were up, he anesthetized himself to the presence of anxious people with a heavy dose, and she accepted a drink. Just to take the edge off, as she continued to feel each vibration through her seat, every squeak and rumble. She fell asleep, but woke in the early hours and looked out to see a bright spiderweb of lights across a dark land. Iceland? Greenland? Ireland? The lights were nothing compared to the glory of the stars above them, thick as snowflakes, icy and steady above the clouds and industrial spewings. The beauty had held her attention, let her fears and concerns ebb away. They were going to Ireland — to her homeland, too, the Taylors being mutts of British ancestry including Irish. Even the landing through rain hadn't stirred her to anxiety.

But getting into Dublin did. The driver was a silent young man who definitely wasn't Irish. They were on the wrong side of the road, exits on the left which should be the passing lane. Everything seemed too close, too fast, the signs for Ballymun and Swords but also McDonald's. The factories and homes looked little different from ones on the outskirts of Charleston. It was indeed very green, but not any more than the West Virginia hills. She could hear the first bars of the official state song, not the John Denver one.

They crossed a river and traveled side streets to a small hotel. It was neat and homey, advertised as a Victorian-era manse for the nearby Anglican Church, and that suited them well. Inside, the plump chairs were comfortable and the proprietress was solicitous and quick to get them settled in a room.

"Now the kettle's right there, with all you'll be needing, and some biscuits," she said. "Breakfast's full Irish, downstairs in the dining room."

She saw a metal kettle but no burner, turned it around in her hands until she saw the plug-in. An electric kettle. They drank lots of tea here, so of course. Which should make Darrick happy. She paged through the colorful stack of teas until she found a decaffeinated Earl Grey.

"Would you like some tea?"

He dragged his attention around to focus on her. Still out of it. "Tea?"

He nodded.

"She said there were biscuits but all I see are cookies."

He managed a smile. "That's what they call them. Biscuits."

"Well, that's just weird. So what do they call biscuits?"

"Scones."

The kettle hummed and she fixed him a cup, and made coffee for herself from a tube of dehydrated crystals.

They were neither one of them good for much, but the articles she'd read said you should get out and do something to clear the jet lag out of your head. After a short nap, they dutifully cleaned up and went out, following the tourist map, walking down to a commercial strip where they wandered through trinket shops, glanced into betting parlors. *Like zombies,* Lourana thought.

A late lunch was fish and chips in a dark pub where the lone patron was absorbed in a televised soccer game. The food was familiar enough, and very good. Everything seemed to be at a smaller scale, the tables tiny, the chairs narrow, as though being on an island made it necessary to use space effectively. They followed a route down into the main part of the city, crossed a bridge that everyone was taking pictures of, and found a bookstore. The Winding Stair. Darrick perked up at last. He gathered books like he was at a one-tripthrough buffet.

"Good thing we're getting a car," she said.

He smiled and added another. From the spines she could see they were all about Irish history and ancient monuments.

Lourana picked up a book of must-see sites in Ireland. All she knew for sure was the Blarney Stone that everyone talked about and a couple of places where they filmed movies, castles and the Cliffs of Moher. And she definitely wanted to ride in one of those little pony-carts.

They straggled back to the hotel with a sack of apples and licorice to balance the tote full of books. The rain that had greeted them at the airport was back again, after reducing to a fine mist during the middle of the day. It was chillier that she expected, so a fire crackling in the parlor was welcome. They spent the afternoon reading and dozing.

She'd read stories where they said the character was "asleep before her head hit the pillow." Lourana always thought was hokum. But when she woke for breakfast, still half in her clothes, she couldn't remember even getting into bed.

Chapter 11

And so they tracked them. And found their trail. It was not so difficult. The Kavanaghs had no lack of lieutenants, still.

Eamon was insistent that they be found. Rory could not deny him. *You never could.*

The sheriff was a blunt instrument but useful. He'd located the place where they'd been staying in Charleston and dispatched a pair of deputies to check it out. It was the lawyers, however, who were most useful. And the congressman, whose name opened doors at agencies where people should have said no. They followed electronic trails and learned that Lourana had, of all things, applied for a passport.

Darrick I could believe, Eamon growled, *but not her.*

Whether it was the strength of Cormac's passion or on his own behalf, Rory couldn't say, but he continued to cultivate Dreama while he labored in the morass of KCL's finances. With his recommendation, she found a new job with a wealth management firm at the office park outside of town.

He sympathized with her, truly. She had lost both her mother and father, in a way. As he guessed people would say he had as well, so he understood her deep loneliness. When he met up with her for coffee one morning, he found her silently weeping and reached for her hand, sensing how his fingers subtly realigned to Cormac's grip. He stroked her shoulder and she kittened up to that comfort. Eamon stayed silent.

"You miss your mother?"

She sniffled and nodded. At Eamon's prodding, but with Cormac's voice, he asked about where Lourana might be going. Even Cormac's gentle words weren't able to pry loose what wasn't there to be found. All she knew was that her mother was taking a long, well-deserved vacation.

"Where do you think she might go? Has she ever said anything about traveling?"

"Not really. She did like Mexican food and joked about going there someday. Eating tacos until she busted a gut."

Eamon was chagrined. If they went south, they could cross anywhere over thousands of miles.

"She checks in with me every day," Dreama added.

"That's good." Rory found himself asking, "Is she happy?"

"I don't know. Darrick can be a scary person, but she seems to have set all that aside. I think she really loves him, but what if he does something, gets out of control?"

He was, still, an unknown quantity. Cormac.

Those who answered to the Kavanaghs maintained a wide and sensitive web, waiting for Darrick or Lourana to blunder across and alert them. Finally, like a vibration traveling from a struggling moth to the spider, came verification on a flight manifest from Philadelphia to Dublin.

You must go after them. Eamon.

We'll have no rest til he's ended, cried Old Scratch.

Our homeland, source of all we are. That voice was hardly even heard. Padraig, who had dug the first mine.

Why not let him go? The others rose in fury and shouted Cormac down.

Rory realized he was sitting at his desk, head in his hands, fingers tearing at his hair like a figure from an old horror movie.

Chapter 12

She thought Darrick looked stunned (again) but for Lourana, this "full Irish breakfast" was a wonder to behold. Fried eggs, a strange slab of cured meat, a black round of something that resembled fried liver mush, potatoes, a thick slice of bread with butter and jam, sliced tomatoes. The beans were a bit odd; still, she tucked into her plate with gusto, while Darrick poked at the unfamiliar bits.

"Do you know what this is?"

She shrugged. "It's not what I thought. Some kind of sausage."

"That would be our black pudding, m'dear," said the hostess, arriving with a pot of tea.

"Is it — pork?" Darrick asked.

"Well, yes. The better part is blood, with suet and oatmeal to hold it together. And herbs for flavor."

Darrick carefully bypassed the black disc in favor of the eggs.

"I really thought it was liver mush," she confided.

"And that would be better?"

"You're just like Dreama, won't try anything that you can't get at the drive-through at McDonald's." Lourana took another bite, just to make her point, though Darrick eyed her as though she was a carnivorous beast in the zoo.

Though she avoided the beans and he the sausage, they were both "full as ticks, as Pap would say," when they went out to wander some more.

They had a tourist map with the places to see — Phoenix Park, Dublin Castle, the statue of Molly Malone, Guinness Storehouses, the emigration museum. The streets were lined with betting shops and small stores, the windows full of lace and thick sweaters and silver. Musicians played on stoops and street corners, with fiddles and squeezeboxes and tin whistles. Some of the tunes were familiar to Lourana as ones that had been carried to the mountains of America. For a time, in the midst of all this excitement, she set aside her worry about why they had fled to this distant place, charming though it might be.

After crossing the river by the Ha'Penny Bridge and returning on the O'Connell, they wandered down through a shopping district until they found a bench on the edge of a park near a military memorial.

A lean man wearing rimless glasses and an out-of-date suit was telling a story about a young ne'er-do-well who was out walking late at night and was set upon by a troop of fairies bearing a corpse. She bent forward to hear his words above the traffic.

"Teig O'Kane hasn't a word for us, no, not three times asked, so now he will pay for his wicked life by becoming our slave. Lift up that corpse we were carrying."

"Do you want . . ." Darrick began, but she shushed him as the storyteller told about how the corpse was set on his back, "and had a tight hold upon him so that he could no more shake it off than a horse its tight-girthed saddle." Teig was tasked with finding a churchyard that would allow him to enter and bury this body before the dawn. So through the night he wandered from place to place, each time being rejected by the bodies already there, and the corpse clutched at him and spoke into his ear, "Bury me, bury me in the burying-ground."

Lourana thought about the books she'd read as a girl, The *Tell-Tale Lilac Bush* and *Coffin Hollow,* stories of ghosts from the hills and hollows of West Virginia. Those books were constantly being stolen from the libraries, she remembered, *because they were our own tales, not some mocking story made up about us.*

She shuddered to think of the Kavanagh clan, how the bones of their ancestors were laid out in the coal crypt beneath their mansion. What kind of souls did they have, that neither went to their reward nor rotted away with the corpse but stayed on, haunting the living. Eamon speaking through his son's mouth. Generations riding the living, feeding on those who fell across their path.

"Young Teig was a changed man, and stopped his drinking and carousing and losing at cards, and especially wandering about at nights for ceilidhs," the storyteller said. "And he wed Mary and it's well known he was a happy man in his marriage and all the days of a very long life."

As the applause spattered away, Lourana dropped a couple of coins into a brimmed hat upturned at his feet. He glanced at her and gave a cockeyed grin, which made Lourana blush. Perhaps she'd given too little. More likely, too much. She could not get the hang of the hard money here.

"You know that was a 20 Euro coin you dropped," Darrick confirmed. "Plus."

"Oh. Sorry."

"That's a good hourly rate for street corner busking."

She wasn't going to apologize again, either for being clueless or for being generous.

"I was going to ask you what you wanted to do for dinner, but you were far too enchanted with the storyteller." He was not looking at her, instead, he surveyed the park as he spoke.

"Sorry," she said, and thought about how many times she had said that in her life, to everyone, as though just her breathing was somehow offensive. "I mean, yes, I am getting hungry. What do you think?"

He turned to face her and she could see now that he was holding his irritation in check, see it in the set of his mouth and how his gray eyes were shadowed.

"Ah, what a lovely couple! Would you like me to take your photo?" The woman held up one of those instant photo cameras. Her hair was green, matching her dress.

"No." Darrick was up and moving away.

"Uh, no thank you," Lourana said, and followed his rapid retreat into the park.

She was puffing a bit by the time she caught up with him, near the center of the park and far from the tourist throng.

"What's wrong?"

"Have you forgotten why we're here? That this is not a simple vacation?"

"No, I haven't forgotten," she said, though she had, briefly, occasionally.

"Then why would you let someone take our picture?" He was agitated now, even beginning to sway a bit as his ataxia reawakened.

"You didn't have to be rude to her."

"And you need to pay attention!" Lourana saw the stares as Darrick was nearly shouting.

"Then maybe you would like to calm down so everyone in Dublin isn't looking at you."

He poked at his glasses, a familiar tic, then turned abruptly and walked away across the park, without looking back. Lourana felt shudders run up her arms and a tightness in her throat. They'd disagreed over things, these months, but after the horrors they'd met and overcome, this kind of petty argument had seemed impossible. Darrick was out of sight, and she didn't know whether to follow or stay put.

She walked a little ways following his path, then sat down on a bench beside a lake where swans floated.

An old woman all in black, with a black hat perched on her wispy white hair, a black shawl draped around her shoulders against the early spring chill, was feeding pigeons out of a paper sack. She scattered breadcrumbs and cooed to them as they fluttered down. Lourana wondered if she was a widow, as she seemed, or just someone playacting. There were so many of that kind of performers on the streets, but her dress did not seem to be a costume, and her welcoming of the birds not an act.

It had been a while, though Lourana could not have said how long, when she heard the familiar slur of Darrick's feet on the pavement. He said nothing, just sat down, took her hand and waited.

So they'd patched things up, but the pressure of their situation did not ease. Lourana was so deeply aware they'd never had a time of easy relaxation, of getting to know each other.

And neither one of us is an easy person to get to know.

They had a bit of lunch, then went back to the room. She was still aching from the argument, knowing she'd been wrong about the picture but not willing to say so given his reaction. Finally, Darrick announced he was taking a nap. He knew she had a Zoom chat set with Dreama, and avoided mentioning it as he yawned and pulled down the covers.

She checked the time, just after 5:30 pm in Redbird, and slipped out quietly to use the visitor PC in the lobby. An electric fire glowed red and in the dining room, she could see the table was set for breakfast.

"Hi Momma," Dreama greeted her.

"Hey baby."

"Are you having a good time? Seeing all the sights?"

"Mostly just relaxing." Lourana had tried to keep their whereabouts hazy, though Dreama kept asking, so she told her they were touring Europe, "One of those if-this-is-Tuesday-it-must-be-Belgium package deals." That seemed close enough to the truth but far off the mark. She ached at the weight of the secrets she carried.

"Drinking a lot of tea?"

She laughed at that. Darrick was certainly having his share, but Lourana had yet to develop a taste for it.

Dreama's head was bent. She was looking at her phone.

"Everything okay with you?"

She was slow to answer, rising up to respond like a fish coming up from deep water. Something had her attention, and it wasn't Lourana.

"Everything okay?"

"Oh, sure!" She flashed that quick smile, her father's dimple, and Lourana felt relieved to see it. And the bright blue jacket and floral printed blouse she was wearing, instead of the somber clothing that had marked her mourning for Cormac.

Something has changed.

Chapter 13

It was a magnificent hotel, like a jewel box built to encase priceless artifacts. Rory watched the sun glint off its metal panels as he followed the GPS toward the Docklands. Right now he didn't care about the architectural provenance of his hotel, just a room, a bed, and the surcease that sleep brought from the tumult in his skull.

Of all the inhabitants of his mind, only Eamon was enthralled by the idea of Ireland, almost sentimental in his responses to place-names in Gaelic and the omnipresent green. He'd been the one who'd years ago commissioned the genealogical investigations, the creation of a family tree, discovery of the family crest. The house, once just "the Kavanagh mansion," was rechristened Knockaulin House after the hill-fortress of the Kavanagh kings on Cnoc Ailinne. His own father and grandfather had not cared for legends, focusing their energies on producing coal, always the coal. Strangely, the only true Irishman in the lot, immigrant Padraig who'd picked and shoveled his way into the Pittsburgh seam, was almost silent about their arrival on the Old Sod.

The room was beautifully appointed and the welcome amenities posh. Rory kicked off his shoes, threw his clothes across the nearest chair, and plunged naked into linen sheets that smelled of meadow flowers.

He woke famished, his mouth dry and skin tight as if he'd been sojourning in a desert. He'd come to recognize this kind of need, one that a steak wouldn't satisfy nor alcohol damp down.

He changed into running gear, including a hooded windbreaker against the damp chill, laced up his comfortable old running shoes, and went out into the Dublin night.

He angled toward Merrion Square Park for a loosening jog, setting a pace that stretched cramped muscles and pushed the jet lag from his brain. The paths were wide, trees heavy with water dripping over couples strolling under shining umbrellas. Rain came down soft but steady, and his face became wet and his hands. But no physical sensation, pleasurable or otherwise, was going to help.

He passed Oscar Wilde stretched on his stone, the elongated limbs reminding him of some painting. An odalisque? A Descent from the Cross?

After a couple of circuits, he could deny Eamon no longer. He angled past the National Museum toward the congested streets of Temple Bar. Ordinarily he'd avoid such tourist quarters, with their milling crowds and noise and smell of spilled beer and vomit, but tonight was different. There were nooks and alleys where people did business they didn't want seen. Drugs, sex. He watched a college-age man in a rugby scarf as he catcalled and sprayed lewd invitations at women. When the Guinness sent him reeling down a sideway after a place to piss, Rory followed.

He stood slightly behind as the man fumbled at his crotch.
"Excuse me."
He turned, doughy face twisted in a scowl. "Feck off, you."
Rory was disgusted by him, the uncleanness of both body and spirit, but Eamon did not care. He grasped the man on the shoulder, between heart and head, pulling him close so that they were intimate as lovers. Where Rory would have taken only a bit of nourishment, Eamon's greed drew the man's life force quickly across the narrow gap, energy that expanded in Rory's body, in every tissue and ligament, every cell. The victim was a lout, without question, but Rory would have left him with only a day-long fatigue that he'd have accepted as

a normal part of a raging hangover. Eamon's overriding hunger consumed the man's life, however, and left his depleted body slumped like a sack of old clothes against the mossy wall.

Rory backed away, replete but repulsed by what he, they, we, had done. Unlike the paternal transfer, these feedings were only energy, nothing more. Nothing of the memory and personality. He wondered what became of the spirit.

Rain beaded on his jacket and pants; it did not penetrate, but a chill reached his legs and back as though he'd soaked in the man's blood. He pulled the hood lower, mingled with the crowd, and made his way back to the hotel.

The doorman met him with an umbrella and took his jacket. The concierge held out a soft wrap to gather up the wet and spoke into his ear as they moved toward the elevators. "The Garda called for you. They wish you to know the party you seek has arrived."

Chapter 14

There was time enough.

The Garda said that Darrick and Lourana were scheduled to pick up a car late in the day, in Dublin City Center, and Rory had stopped by the agency to check. Who would have thought, a chance encounter with old acquaintances so far away from the small town of Redbird? Such fun, the clerk had said.

There would be time then to finish the task a hapless deputy had failed to accomplish last fall. That man was no longer at the department. He went deer hunting and was never heard from again, his body never found. KCL had contributed handsomely to a relief fund for his family.

Now Eamon, having satisfied himself with plans for the surprise attack, was content to wait quietly.

Relieved of the most intrusive of his forefathers, Rory was free to do as he wished, which on this dreary morning began with a walk round the National Library. Later, he planned a visit to the National Museum of Archaeology in its mirror-image building across the plaza.

As he walked into the colonnaded entrance, he felt Cormac's light touch on his thoughts, a graceful thanks.

Rory had the requisite exposure to the humanities allowed in a business curriculum, but Cormac's intense response as they moved through the displays communicated a steady flow of emotion and commentary. He longed to touch the books, hold them in his hands, or rather, his uncle did, but Rory was finding that most of his thoughts and emotions were shared, whether with one, two, three others. Sometimes he did not know whose desires he was inhabiting, or was inhabited by. Only when he was running did he feel complete, whole.

Cormac's excitement increased as they approached the darkened entrance to the Yeats exhibit. Banners above them carried photos of the poet's bespectacled face, young to old and back, with hair falling over one brow. Family groups and a tapestry of Innisfree, documents about Irish nationalism, harps, photos of women who were lovers or patrons or both, brown ink on brown paper, theater programs — it was a kind of cult, Rory thought, how the nation had accumulated all this material. Then the spiritualism and Golden Dawn, a puppet theater bordered by gaudy tarot cards — it really seemed over the top.

A voice like surf, rolling and retreating, intoning poetry. Rory followed into a room where handwritten lines were cast on a scrim, and the voice continued,

> *A tattered coat upon a stick, unless*
> *Soul clap its hands and sing, and louder sing . . .*

Other figures moved beyond the display cases, there and gone. Reflections. Shadows. Ghosts.

Yeats believed in ghosts, Cormac shared, *and thought they continued hating and loving the same, souls committing the same acts of heroism or atrocity over and over again.*

He felt a certain disquiet.

> *Consume my heart away; sick with desire*
> *And fastened to a dying animal*
> *It knows not what it is; and gather me*
> *Into the artifice of eternity.*

Rory felt a whole-body rush, like bitter cold that registers as fire, as though he'd been submerged in an icy sea. The line flared again and again in his thoughts, "sick with desire and fastened to a dying animal." For the first time, he understood what poetry was, and how his uncle had negotiated a different kind of world shaped by words and images.

> *Once out of nature I shall never take*
> *My bodily form from any natural thing . . .*

As the voice incanted line after line, his awareness and Cormac's drew closer together, embraced if that could be a word to describe formless presence. Through Cormac's awareness, he began to see this poem, each poem, as a key small element in the creation of the world, shaped and necessary though it might be minuscule, overlooked like a jeweled fly on a flower.

This is how I kept my sanity.

Rory shared with him how running, exhausting himself on cross-country treks, had given him a similar refuge.

The boundary between them became an invisible tension, a quivering pane, and at that juncture they drew strength from each other. The elders did not appear, could not be sensed.

Outside Eamon's understanding.

"And the others?"

So it would seem.

After the Yeats, there seemed to be no more attraction in the library for Cormac, and he retreated to brood over the poems while Rory, restless, moved on to the National Museum of Archaeology.

This was another sort of surfeit. Displays of golden torcs for the necks of kings, golden boats, golden pins to fasten their shaggy cloaks against the unceasing rain. Reliquaries containing the bones of putative saints, ancient hollow-eyed heads pecked out of stone. The dead past, preserved and interpreted and safely encased in lucite.

But the bog bodies, they were different.

He spent a long time staring at the crumpled forms, pressed flat and tinted by the bog water. One, a torso sliced off by the mining machine and missing its head as well, was a leather bag, a piece of a saddle, until you saw the hands. Those remained as in life, the fingers gently curled, lines of the palm still visible enough to tell a fortune.

I have seen such, myself. Have cut them from the peat. Padraig.

They were strangled, sacrificed. Cormac.

There was such deep silence in them. Rory wondered, as he did often, if there were others like himself in the world. Like the Kavanagh men. Until his father's felling, he'd been shown little of this legacy, only that he could draw near to people and pull some energy from them, as you'd warm your body by standing next to a fire. Just a bit, scarcely noticed, infrequently tried. A trick when finals were upon him so that he could study longer, though his sense of fair play would not let him use it to win races. If that wasn't performance enhancing, he didn't know what was. Then came the moment when his father, and his father's fathers, weighted his soul with a past like a forged chain still hot from the flames, and the ability, and desire, to take and take and take.

Ghosts? He wished the haunting were a matter of creaking doors and cold drafts. For him, the dead didn't linger in the world but continued on within him, instead of parting from the body for some other destiny or dying with the flesh. This Darrick his family pursued, he was not the same, but what was he? His father's fractured memories showed him his adversary, a creature filled with a different kind of light. He feared him, or Eamon did, yet felt drawn to him.

Rory moved along, barely glancing at most of the exhibits, until he paused in front of the silky curves and gold bosses of the Armagh Chalice, elevated on its pedestal.

I'd drink deep from such a cup. Eamon. *Perhaps we did, when we were kings.*

Rory had read that it was a wine cup for the Mass, not meant for a banqueting hall. But Kavanagh kings, if there were such, might have been heedless enough to claim the holy thing.

Kings we were. When we've completed this task, we'll go to Dún Ailinne and stand on sacred ground.

They left the library in a hurry.

"What's the matter?"

"I saw him." Lourana glanced back over her shoulder even as she was powering ahead.

"Who?"

"Rory Kavanagh."

"Here?"

"I saw him through the gaps between displays. He was just standing and listening."

Darrick's pace quickened as well, taking them out of the open spaces and closed-off buildings of the governmental center. They turned onto Kildare Street and moved along the edge of the flow of people.

"You must be mistaken. How many red-headed Irishmen are there in this place, after all?" He might have been trying to make light of this, but she could feel the undercurrent of his uneasiness.

"It was him. Tall. Skinny. Curly red hair. It was him." Lourana had no doubt. She'd felt his grip that day, soft then becoming hard, looked into his eyes as they became angry and Eamon's voice emerged from his lips.

"What are we going to do?" Darrick slowed and seemed suddenly uncertain of his direction. He surely did not like the crowds swirling around him, the press of emotions that could trigger his protective response.

"We'll get the car, and get the hell out of here."

"It's way too early."

She knew it was, knew that even before church bells began to mark the single stroke of one o'clock. "Maybe it will be ready."

Her wish was fulfilled when they got to the counter and the clerk looked up their reservation, looked it up twice, and confirmed that it was ready and waiting for paperwork and the walk-around. She seemed fidgety as she got the keys and had them read and initial and sign.

"Where would you be heading?"

"We don't know. Just sightseeing," Darrick said. "Why? Is there a mileage limit or more insurance or something?"

"Well, you're not covered if you cross into the UK, Northern Ireland you understand, unless you want to add that. No other limitations." She glanced at Lourana, then Darrick. "It's just, a man was here, asking about your reservation. A friend, he said. Nice-looking young man — you'll meet up then? I wouldn't want you to miss him."

Lourana didn't say anything, but looked sideways at Darrick.

"You're not having any other issues, I'm sure." A question lurked in there.

"No, none," Lourana said. "We'll let our friend know. Is the tank full?"

The clerk reminded them about driving on the left, and the hazards of roundabouts, and warned them about gas being measured in liters and not gallons so don't be surprised, "but a nice little car like this won't weigh heavy on your pocketbook." They noted dents and scratches, which Lourana thought there were all too many of, before the keys finally were handed over and they drove out of the lot. Slowly.

"I guess we won't forget," she said, indicating the huge sticker on the windshield that reminded about driving on the left.

At their lodgings, they provided a hurried excuse for leaving early — the city was too much for them, they needed somewhere quiet.

"Where might you be headed?"

They looked at each other.

"If you've no plans, and you want to get free of the hen parties and tourist buses, I'd suggest County Donegal, so long as you avoid Donegal Town proper. They don't name it the Forgotten County for naught," said the woman. "Or try County Cavan. It's where I grew up. No one goes there, except to catch fish. It's all about cows and rivers and lakes, like your Wisconsin."

Chapter 15

Rory could barely breathe.

He'd spent two hours dawdling over a plate of prawns and grilled vegetables, thick bread with golden butter and a couple of excellent Scraggy Bay ales, watching for Darrick and Lourana to arrive and pick up their econobox. But the scheduled hour approached and passed. When Rory finally went in to check on his "old friends from back home," the clerk said they'd been there quite some time before, sure, hadn't they picked it up early, and no she didn't know their plans. They'd be in touch with him on the cell no doubt. At the B&B, the proprietor gave him a long look-over, then explained the bustle of the city was too much for them, "nervous folks, they are," and they went out to the country, somewhere. She waved toward the west, but then everything was west of Dublin.

And Eamon had exploded. *Now you've let them slip away.*

Rory knew the expression "seeing red," but not until this moment did he understand it so intimately. A red veil wavered over everything, and the world tipped and skidded even as he sat in the quiet seclusion of the parked Mercedes. Only with reminders from Cormac about the plans to visit Dún Ailinne and a fatherly exhortation from Patrick had Eamon calmed enough to restore the normal world.

"They'll alight soon enough," whispered Rory, feeling himself shrink, again the awkward, gangly kid facing his father's scorn.

The Garda will locate them, added Patrick.

Eamon's plans would be set in motion. Track, isolate, eliminate. And then what? Rory wondered, deep in his covert.

Rory took the M9 to R418, as the GPS advised, the hill rising on the right and the round tower of Old Kilcullen ahead on the left. Cnoc Ailinne, the hill crowned by the remains of the old dun, stood in the meadows of the Thompson farm, inaccessible to the public without advance permission but the way had been smoothed, gates swung open so that Rory could drive close. He began to make his way to the summit.

Rain was blowing away toward the east. The rising sun through the edges of the storm arched a rainbow above the intensely green landscape, a sentimental painting. When Rory reached the summit, he found little there of past glories: faint outline of the former walls and some large boulders strewn about.

Eamon's anger had been swept aside like the clouds, and he exulted at the view from the hill and the sense he claimed to have of the presence of the ancient kings. Padraig, too, was active in describing details of areas west and south as he recalled them. But Rory tried to focus his attention on the lay of the land, the hillocks and little streams, thinking how he might approach it as a running course.

With so little to see, interest soon waned even for his father, and Rory started to head down the hill. He thought he could hear drums, and shook away that kind of imagining.

Then he saw a ragged party laboring up the grade, some of them in jeans and T-shirts emblazoned with mottos, others in brown robes that whipped in the wind. As they came closer, he realized the robed ones weren't monks or Christian pilgrims, but pagan enthusiasts, hoods thrown back from shaggy heads, two of them beating time with hand drums. Bodhrán, he remembered. Curiosity made him wait, watching as the group formed a semicircle around a jowly man of middling years with a staff and a medallion swinging on his chest and a robe that was a couple of shades off from white. A priest, he supposed, some kind of druid. The man looked curiously at him, then went into his spiel.

"This was the fortress of Hugony the Great who united the warring tribes of Leinster and became their king." The man swept a pudgy arm to indicate the vista, his sleeve fluttering. "Imagine all this, rich lands as far as you can see, and at the center this holy mountain and at its crown a strong fortress, Dún Ailinne, where we stand now."

Fool and mountebank, Patrick groused. But Cormac's interest was roused, and Eamon's even more.

There was little of the holy man about him, Rory thought, and more of the con man. Still, he could feel a certain power in his words.

"Here kings were made and ruled through the ages, from Cathair Mor through the splitting of the Leinster dynasties north and south. The last Kildare-based king died in 1042 and from that time all the kings of Leinster came from the southern branch, until the last of the Kavanagh kings was defeated in the 17th century by the British."

"But isn't Tara the seat of the kings?" asked one of the civilians, a bit of snark to his voice though he raised his hand like a schoolboy.

"The Uí Néill made up that story, naming Tara as the seat of the High Kings as though none others existed," the leader scoffed. "Other kingdoms had their own sacred places for making their kings. Navan Fort for Ulster, and Rathcroghan for Connacht, and here, the center of the ancient kingdom of Leinster, as is told in the Dindsenches Ard Ruide," and he began to chant in Gaelic.

He's saying that Leinster was a place of great wealth and was held in high regard. Cormac's studies in Gaelic had a practical use.

Seeing the tourists shuffle and look anxious, the leader switched to English, explaining, "The eastern kingdom is a place of wealth, importing silk and wine and other rich goods. The people are blessed, the men being noble in speech and the women exceptionally beautiful."

One of the women laughed and leaned close to another to make a comment.

The gaggle went to consider the scattered boulders, which the priest said were all that remained of a great standing stone called "The Ail," for which the hill was named, "according to legend, thrown here by a giant."

With so little to see, the group began to wander around the crown of the hill, some hugging themselves against the wind, looking down perhaps with longing at the comforts of a sightseeing van covered with giant shamrocks. The leader was turning to go when Eamon came to the fore.

"You mentioned the Kavanagh kings," Rory said, his voice half his own. "The family crest is a leopard lioné above two crescent moons, is it not?"

The man gave him a penetrating stare.

"Yes, that would be correct. How do you come to know that?"

"That insignia is carved on the great fireplace at Knockaulin House, my home. I am a Kavanagh."

"The Kavanaghs are a river rising from many springs, from Carlow and Wexford, assuredly, but others of the name are known in Cork as well, and in County Monaghan. Do you know your forefathers?"

Closer than you'd imagine, thought Rory. "We descend from the king line, according to genealogical studies."

"Then your medieval forefather would have been Domnall, son of Diarmait. He was first to use the Kavanagh surname."

"Indeed."

The man waved to the group, his little flock paused at the edge of the circle, unsure whether to stay or go. They took his instruction and disappeared down the hill toward the van.

"Welcome, then, to your native soil." The man's eyes were small and intense, secreted inside folds of sunless flesh. "But you'd be Americans, if I don't miss my guess, and the immigration not recent."

"Early nineteenth century."

"Kavanaghs were well dispersed around the world by then, the English having broken them as they did all the Celtic nobility. Other lands welcomed their leadership and fighting abilities, from the time of the Stuart kings to the Austro-Hungarian Empire."

Rory felt Eamon's glowing gratification at the confirmation of all he believed about himself, his ancestors.

"Rory Kavanagh," he said, extending his hand.

I named you Padraig, complained Eamon.

"I greet the Red King," the man said, but his grip went further, hand to wrist for a while like some gladiator. "I am Kaava, or as the English pronounce it, Cathbad, as it's spelled. A Forest Sage. You would call me a druid."

"That was what I was thinking."

"Of course." He chuckled. "Like the druids of old, however, I'm quite unbloodied. More philosopher than priest. In my previous work I was a university lecturer."

"So those are your students?"

"The ones wearing robes are students within our grove. Good folk all, but their abilities are uneven. A teacher learns to assess talent, and interest, quickly. Those others are paying guests, merely curious."

His shrewd eyes bored in on Rory's, as though he could sense the braiding personalities that crowded his immaterial thoughts. He had the intensity of a prospector weighing grains of gold dust.

"What brings you to this hill of destiny, my American friend? A quest?"

Rory was not prepared to answer that. *We've come to destroy an enemy,* Eamon said, and Cormac amended, *To find our source.*

"I'm interested in our history," he said. "It's one thing to read about it in a book, another to see the places where it happened."

"You may have found the source of your line," he said, "but it takes more than standing on high ground to claim your inheritance. I feel that you face some barrier. Someone who contends with you."

Darrick, cried Eamon. *He knows about Darrick.*

There was something hypnotic about the man. Rory wondered if he was getting ensnared in some sort of cult, though the man and his followers seemed harmless enough. What had he called himself? Unbloodied.

Patrick continued to complain, but Eamon's enthusiasm drowned out those criticisms and Rory's misgivings. Eamon wanted this. Wanted to pursue his visions of kingship into the past, put something tangible behind the airy tracings of genealogy that purported to extend his line back for thousands of years. Wanted the power to put an end to his enemy.

"Here on this hill, the Kavanagh kings were made in the ancient fashion, standing on the stone."

Rory looked around. The windswept grass offered neither platform nor throne. He wondered why the ancestors who lived within him now went no further than old Padraig, the one who dug the first mine in Redbird, without the presence of any noble progenitor, much less a king.

"We are all temporary on this physical plane. We die and the body quits its struggles, but we are only changed, the soul continuing forward and finding a new home." The druid looked at Rory. "That is our teaching."

My body in the tomb, shall leap into the light lost in my mother's womb. Cormac.

"Do you wish, then, to stand in the footprints of the king? It can be done, at the proper time." Cathbad reached into the folds of his dingy robe and came out with a cellphone. "Let me have your mobile."

Chapter 16

The road took them to Cavan town first, but they found it too busy. The tourism map offered a smaller town up ahead. Killeshandra.

"It reminds me of where I grew up," he told Lourana as they drove into the village. "Spotted cows and little rolling hills."

The Lough Bawn Inn seemed likely, but it was "full of anglers" going out after toothy pike that roamed the lakes like tigers, or so they were told. The desk clerk asked her mother, and she knew a woman, and so they found a room in a rambling old stucco house overlooking a lake and herds of grazing dairy cows.

The woman who'd opened her home to the forlorn Yanks accepted payment in folded Euros, asked few questions and answered fewer. "No meals," she'd said gruffly. "No cooking in the room, either. There's a kettle." So for lunch and dinner, they walked down the hill, through the town to the hotel or one of the pubs. Each time, they passed a wall decorated with a giant mural of a high-wheeled cart carrying a single milk can: "One day all the milk of a parish would be churned in the one churn." Prophecy of St. Colmcille. Killeshandra Co-operative

Agricultural Society. There was something both reassuring and a bit alarming in that, Lourana thought, depending how you read it.

The terror of the near-encounter with Rory began to recede as they settled into the slow pace of village life. No train ran near, just a bus from Dublin, and that not direct. This was to be a stopping place, but on the way to where? Donegal? They weren't talking about that right now.

The weather was cool and bright, while in Dublin rain had spattered or drenched at least part of every day. They sat beside the lake and watched swans glide over the water. They went walking in the forest park, where nestled among the roots of trees were tiny elf-houses painted by local children.

"Look, here's one for you." A gold-painted door offered entry to a royal blue cottage inscribed "Darick."

"Close."

"Close enough."

At the pub where they tried bangers and mash for lunch, the bouncy waitress was chatty with tourists as well as locals. "If you'll be staying for a bit, we have the village festival on offer. Skittles and games, jam tasting, all such."

"That sounds lovely," Lourana said, and meant it. She had always enjoyed the Redbird Pepperoni Roll Festival, with booths strung out along the riverside park selling funnel cakes and lemonade and the local specialty in all sizes and shapes. Then the pier collapse erupted in her memory, rescue vehicle lights strobing red and blue across the park and frozen river, the twisted pier hanging above polluted water, the dead. She shivered with the cold of that late November night.

"Why, this very evening — I'd forgot — there'll be a ceilidh at the hall. It's at half seven. Musicians from hereabouts, loads of fun."

"Singing and dancing?" Lourana glanced at Darrick.

"Both on tap. It's at the fine new Killeshandra Community Hall — well, new 10 years gone, but that's new enough around here." She showed them an area map, which was mostly occupied by squiggles and blobs of blue. "You'd be taking the R201, toward the fire station. Can't miss it."

"Ahhh," Darrick began, then halted. He pushed his glasses up on his nose, that familiar gesture. "Half seven?"

"Half past the hour, love. Seven thirty." She gave his shoulder a little pat. "I'll be seeing you there, then?"

On the way home, Lourana accused him of flirting.

"No, really, I wasn't."

"I'm kidding."

"She was just being nice," he protested.

"You're a handsome fella."

Now he became agitated, which got her uncomfortable, too, so she left off. It's not that he didn't have a sense of humor, but he was not used to the rough-and-tumble joshing that passed for affection in her world.

Come 7:30, they headed for the event, though Darrick reminded her, "I'm no singer. Especially no dancer."

"I just want to enjoy the music," she said.

As they came to a roundabout, she could hear him say "Left left left" under his breath. Straight-ahead driving was not so bad, but she imagined that turning the wrong way at a traffic circle was just so hard.

"There's 201."

"Now look for the fire station. Like West Virginia directions," she said. "Go out the pike to where the church burned, then bear left and go a piece."

"You feel at home here."

"I do. The people are kind. And they're close to their families, and the land, though I'm sure a move to some big city would bring them a lot more money." She thought about Dreama, clinging to her memories in Redbird, when the whole world awaited her.

His lack of response made her ache, evidence again of a life built like a rickety bridge over gaps and absences. No parents, no brothers or sisters, acquaintances rather than friends, from what he'd told her. An orphan pushed into the world like an unfledged bird to make his way. She remembered how bereft, how hapless he'd seemed when he stumbled into her sweepstakes parlor, stinking of the bone pit that he had been meant never to escape. And then the appearance of a psychic power he didn't understand, a terrible and unwanted gift that left a police officer twisted and dead in the snow, and later another.

She'd been scared, of course, but kept hanging on to hopes of finding Dreama, then to a growing belief in that quiet, decent man who'd asked for her help. And then, of course, his curse or gift or both ended up saving them from the malign force the Kavanaghs had exerted on the people and land for generations.

They found the community center, as promised, a plain beige block building, two stories tall. Music spilled out into the parking lot and carried them inside, to a open room where a low stage was filled by musicians with familiar fiddles and guitars, but also accordions and flat drums and bagpipes that were smaller than she'd pictured, held under the arm and worked like a bellows.

An old man was singing, his hands clasped before him as he told of his love for a Cavan girl, and walking the twelve miles from Killeshandra to have a few hours in the bright summer of her smile. Though he was bent and almost bald, she could hear the young man in his voice.

They got some drinks and found a table to one side of the stage. The music cycled through dance tunes and ballads. Musicians left the stage and others took their places. Couples danced, and solos, and kids in circles, sometimes doing the kind of step-dancing she associated with "Riverdance."

"That fiddler is real good," she said, nodding toward the black-haired man whose face was knotted with the intensity of his playing.

"I thought so, too."

The waitress from the pub spotted them and came over, gushed over their presence at the ceilidh, then spun away to chat with others. Lourana saw her approach the stage and speak with the guitarist, who got up and made his way to the standing microphone.

"Good to see you out here tonight, my friends. We've all brought in our bit of music, and the ladies those cakes that are keeping us fat." A roar of laughter and glasses lifted in a toast. "We've visitors as well tonight, I hear, that have come all the way from the States to take part in our ceilidh."

Darrick whispered, "Oh, no."

"Now, I don't know if they're Irish, but at the Killeshandra ceilidh, everyone is Irish and everyone has a song."

Darrick shook his head.

"It's share and share alike," added the accordion player.

Lourana saw Darrick stiffen, draw into himself, and thought she'd better do something and right quick.

"I'll sing for you," she said, standing to a round of applause and walking to the stage.

"What would you favor us with?" the guitarist asked.

Suddenly, all she could think of was "Danny Boy," then "MacNamara's Band." Good God she couldn't sing those here. But then she remembered "Long Black Veil."

"I'm not used to doing this," she apologized to the band. "Do you know the song 'Long Black Veil'?"

"A bit," said the fiddler. "You go on and we'll find you."

She began on her own, her voice soft, holding the microphone stand and closing her eyes to remember the verses.

First the fiddle came in, plaintive as the lonely winds in a graveyard, then the guitar, the musicians catching hold of the melody.

The story filled her with a swell of homesickness. The chorus about the woman who walks the hills, shrouded and alone, and the verses telling of the man who loved her to his downfall. The fiddler came to her side and his strings quavered like a condemned man's voice. She glanced over. He was a handsome man, his eyes merry as Steve's had been in the good times.

When the song was over, people applauded and Lourana felt a blush creep across her face. She stepped away from the microphone, turning to leave, but the fiddler was in her path.

"You've having me on," he said.

She must have showed her confusion, as he added, "You're a professional. A singer. Where are you from?"

"The United States."

He offered a quizzical smile and a nod, go on.

"A little place in a little state. West Virginia. I don't know if you've ever heard of it."

"Oh, you're a Mountain Mama!" shouted the accordion player, and ran a quick few notes of "Take Me Home, Country Roads."

He motioned her back to the mic and she was ready to sing, now, this song, the one she knew in every fiber of her being.

I'm a miner's lady, she thought, *yes indeed.*

She was shocked to hear what seemed like everyone in the place singing along on the chorus.

An old man began to dance, what she'd have called flatfooting, and Lourana added a few steps of her own.

A raucous cheer echoed in the big room.

Tears began to flow as she sang about her home, the ridges one after the other fading to blue, far away from this pleasant but foreign place. She remembered the highway signs, Wild Wonderful West Virginia, and how a lump always came to her throat when she crossed under one.

One last extra chorus and the song ended. This time, the fiddle player drew her into a powerful hug, his violin held above them like a trophy, and she felt his lips trace a path across her throat.

She looked over his shoulder and saw Darrick, looking hurt and angry. She felt a sudden rush of love, and just a whisper of fear.

Chapter 17

The room was small but they'd put as much distance between the two of them as it would allow. He sat stiffly in the rickety armchair, engrossed in an oversized illustrated volume of Irish history. She had gotten into her nightgown and tucked into the bed, pretending to read about leprechauns.

They'd come back from the ceilidh in silence. She tried a couple of conversation starters, pointing out a still lake under a slice of moon, then how a stone bridge arched over a stream, but he was distant and answered in monosyllables. She'd watched the set of his jaw. Unmoving. *Stubborn, like Mama would have said.*

Lourana got up and put on the kettle, thinking a cup of chamomile was supposed to help settle jangled nerves, but he was having none of it. She fixed herself a cup anyway, the spoon clanking harder against the china than intended, and he glanced up and then away. She added more sugar than she needed, to cover the grassy taste, and choked it down.

I haven't done a damn thing wrong, she thought. *I didn't make that happen, and anyway, it was just a moment. The man got carried away. Nothing to it.*

It was hard not to compare Darrick with Steve right about now. For all her ex's problems, and there had been plenty, he'd never frozen her out in an argument. They'd yell and stomp around and get it out, not brood over it and make the whole world go black.

"Are you going to stay hateful?" she asked.

He glanced over the top of the book but said nothing.

"I'm not going to apologize for nothing, if that's what you're waiting for."

"I didn't ask for an apology."

"Well it was about the most innocent thing you could ask for. I didn't know they were going to ask us to sing. I only volunteered because I knew you were getting antsy."

"I had good reason," he said, and carefully set the book face down on his lap. "We don't need to be showing ourselves off in public. People talking about the Americans, about the songs from West Virginia."

Lourana could have admitted that was true enough, but she was hot now at his superior attitude and plowed right ahead. *The only way out is through, or we'll just break.*

"You think the Kavanaghs wouldn't have some easier way to find us than scouting out a local jam session in the boondocks? Really?"

"I'm sure they do. I think about it all the time. Every waking minute, and most of the night. Where can we go? What should we do?"

He spoke like a wooden man, immobile, no emotion in his face or movement in his body. She wondered if he feared he would lose control if he allowed himself to move.

"We keep on running, but we aren't any closer to finding out anything about your situation. Where your people are from. What that thing is you do. You're reading all those books but have you learned a blessed thing?"

"If there was anything to find out, I want to do that, but good grief, Lourana, how am I supposed to get hold of nothing? Of no history? Of a name that may be random and nothing more?"

He began to get animated. She could feel a little gooseflesh crawl on her arms.

"It's not nothing," she shot back. "The Kavanaghs didn't think it was nothing. Maybe you don't really want to know your ancestry. Maybe that's why we're just wandering."

"Why are you pushing me?"

Lourana glared back. "Because it might could be you need pushing, to make an effort, because the Kavanaghs aren't going to give up and you'd best be strong when they find us and maybe that means finding out why you're the way you are."

She could see his right hand begin to tremble. If he stood, she was sure, he'd be staggering.

"You aren't even trying to shield me from your anger," he accused. "Why are you doing this? Do you want to see if I'll lose control? Do you think I'll hurt you?"

Lourana scrambled to find those mental defenses she'd long ago abandoned, with him. The ones that had protected her from the Kavanaghs. Remembering the terrible intimacy of the moment she'd dropped those defenses with him. Trusting him completely.

Why am I doubtful now?

"You have so much power . . ."

"Yes, and? If I had a gun do you think I'd shoot you? If I had a knife in my hand do you think I'd stab you?"

"No."

"Then why do you doubt me?" His eyes gleamed, maybe from unshed tears. "I can feel that, you know. How you get irritated with me. Like how I push my glasses up when I don't need to. I never had ones that fit until I was an adult. It's a tic. I'm sorry."

"I'm sorry."

"It's nothing." He waved it away. "Worse is how you have these little spasms of fear sometimes."

Lourana flushed with shame.

"I don't meant to."

He made a little sound.

"I don't really, fear you, it's just sometimes everything around us so strange. Sometimes it's good, we're having fun together, but mostly it's like I'm in a dark forest and I wonder what's going to jump out of the bushes at us."

"I'm still waiting for an answer." He spoke slowly and deliberately. "Lourana, do you think I'll hurt you?"

"I don't think you'd ever deliberately, Darrick. But do you have control? Complete control?"

"Haven't you seen these weeks how much control I've gained? The airport? The crowds in the street?"

She thought of his many silences and how he sometimes turned inward to become inaccessible, remote. Those had been moments when he'd had to control his wild and lethal defensive talent. But he'd learned. He wasn't any longer the victim of his empathy, slammed by powerful emotions that others projected, lashing out in return.

"I think you do."

"But you're not sure."

Lourana couldn't lie. He'd know. He'd feel her doubts because she'd once opened herself entirely to him and had not maintained the psychic wall to conceal her fears.

Darrick said nothing, but she saw before he raised the book in front of his face that the tears brimming his eyes had begun to fall.

She felt numb. Shame and fear had turned into a kind of cold fog over her thoughts.

I've hurt the one I love. Who loves me.

She pulled back the covers and got into bed, turning to the wall and pulling the blankets up around her ears.

Sometime in the night, he came to bed. The old bed was hollow at its middle, where someone had slept alone for a very long time. Although she tried to maintain her place close to the edge, she felt herself sliding backward down that slope to the center where he'd also been pulled like a magnet.

They touched.

Chapter 18

Lourana looked at the cheap little phone in her hand and thought again it was a marvel. *Something to use and throw away, but it can carry my voice all the way to West Virginia.*

She sat on a tree stump by the pasture fence, waiting on Dreama, comforted by the slow presence of the cows. They chewed through the lush grass and wildflowers, and their tails switched, and occasionally one would toss back its heavy head to chase away a fly. The smell of their bodies and cow plops drawing flies in the sun made her remember a visit to some relative or other, up in Preston County, fields of buckwheat and daisy-strewn pastures with the same blackand-white cows turning grass into milk.

The phone buzzed and she picked up right away.

"Hi. How's my girl?"

"Hi Momma. I'm good. Working, you know."

"I hope you're doing more than working."

"Not really. You know, Redbird. Not much going on here."

"That's a good reason for you to get out." Lourana could hear herself getting sharp. "You could go on back to Charleston, where you have friends. Someplace with more life for a young woman."

Dreama sighed. "I really don't want to do anything much."

She could sense her daughter's mood, right through the microwaves or whatever, the satellites, just like she was sitting beside her. "You sound like you're down again. Did you break up with that guy you were seeing?"

"Not exactly. He's away on a business trip."

"Oh." Lourana thought that sounded like an excuse for a break-up, but since Dreama had never told her who the guy was, then maybe it wasn't all that significant. "This guy — is he special? Someone you care about?"

"It's complicated."

"I guess. I guess you're not going to give me any more than that." Lourana was glad she'd gone outside to wait for the call. This kind of stuff made Darrick crazy. "He's not some lowlife, is he? At least you've moved on from Cormac."

Nothing.

She was going to go there anyway. "You used to share everything with me, Dreama, at least til you got in with the Kavanaghs."

"Momma, let's not. Please."

"But I'm worried . . ."

"I'm worried about you, too," Dreama said, cutting her off. "Where are you, anyway? When are you coming home?"

"There's no hurry, is there?"

That wasn't any kind of answer. Lourana wondered why she was still keeping this back. What would it hurt to say they were in Ireland? Maybe she was holding out because Dreama was. Tit for tat.

Now that's just ugly.

"Hey baby. I'm in Ireland right now. Maybe not for long. But right now."

"Thank you for telling me. At least I know what side of the globe you're on." Dreama paused. "How's Darrick?"

"He's doing fine."

"You don't sound so sure."

"No, really. We're having fun, seeing the sights. He's just — odd. You know Darrick."

"He's more than odd, I'd say. I wonder if you're safe."

Now Lourana was starting to feel miffed. "Of course. How can you say that? He saved your life!"

"Well, you did, too."

"We both did. Together. But I sure couldn't have done it myself. I don't want to think about what would have happened if he hadn't found us."

"You're right," Dreama admitted.

Long silence. Lourana heard a bird call from the trees behind her, and another answer, like no bird that she knew.

"Momma, are you happy?"

"I'm the one's supposed to be asking that."

Chapter 19

Stand in the footprints of a king.

Rory could hear Eamon mulling over those words, a steady loop like an earworm you can't shake.

You he called the Red King.

Rory knew that signified nothing. His name, Ruiadri in Gaelic, meant "the red king," and no more. He had no illusions.

We might come from another line, whispered Cormac. *From Patrick Kavanagh, the great poet.*

Eamon derided his brother's affections. *An ignorant farmer, who wrote about walking behind a plow.*

Their sibling argument simmered in the background until Rory asserted himself, arguing that, lacking better direction without news of Darrick nor contact from the druid, they might as well see the countryside. Why not the home of the poet? So he found himself driving north and west from Dublin, to County Monaghan like a fist sunk into the gut of Northern Ireland.

Eamon retreated, sulking about this "wild goose chase" but also because the Garda, after an initial favor to the visitor, was proving to be less compliant than his creatures back in Carbon County.

Rory had been impelled, *compelled,* before they left Dublin to demand that police find out where the couple had traveled. "You have traffic cameras, correct?" he asked, quelling the rumble that threatened to overcome his voice.

"And what is your interest in these people? Do you have a complaint? Is there criminal activity?"

"They're friends. We've lost touch with them."

The sergeant gave him a look. "Private citizens have the right to be let alone, even by their friends. If they're genuinely pining after your company, I imagine they'll be in touch."

It was all Rory could do to nod and walk out of the room, knowing he couldn't speak again. Eamon was raging to take control and right there, within the police station, grasp the man's life and pull it from his body. They had nothing now but the information on their quarries' return tickets from Dublin, which offered the assurance that they would catch up to them at that time if not before. He walked with careful attention down the steps, his body not entirely his own, got in his car and locked the doors. Had he been locking them against a danger from outside or within?

The highway was an easy drive, the urban face of Dublin giving way to suburbs and then to countryside, a landscape tessellated with squares of crops and pasture, overlooked by squadrons of wind turbines turning long arms in the sea wind. Exits peeling off to the left for Drogheda and ancient sites such as Kells and Newgrange. When he left the highway for smaller roads, he could on each side look down lanes high-banked with hedges.

Cormac's excitement made him the loudest voice in the lineage as they approached Inniskeen, boyhood home of the poet.

This is just as he described it, not beautiful but not ugly, just a place where people worked the land until the "stony gray soil of Monaghan," broke them, Cormac quoted.

They arrived at the church with its one stark tower, now home to the literary center that had images of the poet like those of Yeats in Dublin, a face similarly bespectacled but with a nose like a potato that showed he was of the earth, nothing ethereal about him. It overlooked a graveyard with ranks of mold-spotted tombstones squared inside a wall. Rory — actually, Cormac — meditated for a long moment in front of a simple wooden cross bearing a plaque, the poet's signature, and a line of his verse.

A couple of men nearby turned away from the grave. "The one good thing about County Monaghan, it's said, is the path you take to leave it." The other answered, "Aye." Rory was familiar with that kind of terrible attachment, how the people of Carbon County and indeed much of Appalachia were torn between their love of the green hills and a knowledge of how their lives were being sacrificed each day they remained.

Cormac urged him along the Patrick Kavanagh Trail to the old parish hall, the round tower, the railway bridge, then back. As Rory stood at the junction and studied the six-kilometer route, the prospect of a good lope caught hold, and he realized how he'd allowed family business to overwhelm his own needs. Street clothes were not suitable for running; still, he stretched, then started a slow jog down the trail, enjoying the feel of his muscles extending and his blood moving through his body.

The trail took him past a crossroads to the Kavanagh homestead, a bare gray-faced farmstead, three windows on each floor and a dark green door facing the road. He slowed to a walk as he passed by another monument, and then a farm brewery, Brehon. The name sent a little shudder through them all. Jogging again, he made the turn by the old school, passed arched stone bridges and broken stone houses and a sign for "Rocksavage Estate" and a hill called Shancoduff. *The name of a poem,* Cormac noted, *and Inniskeen Road as well.*

Rory turned back toward the village. His uncle clutched after other places, other names, but he wasn't about to visit them all. He'd brought Cormac here, given him his wish, but this was as much legend as his father's fantasies of kingship, all a gauzy veil over the reality of blood and bone and breath. Billy Brennan's whitewashed barn where dances had been held, *"the wink-and-elbow language of delight,"* whispered Cormac. The view of Slieve Gullion over a panorama of land where the hero Cú Chullain had roamed. The triangular field where the poet had endlessly labored like a figure out of Greek myth.

But a jog was not a run, did not ease his internal chatter, Eamon and his fathers deriding this branch of Kavanagh history none of them believed meant anything to them, not even Cormac.

But it might be possible. Cormac, whose attention had been outward, responded to Rory's thoughts of him.

"No more than the druid's fairy tales," Rory answered, even as he eased his stride to a walk in response to his uncle's longing. He took the linking path back to the circuit, the round tower and the church tower standing as landmarks for the end. As he stood beside the car, Eamon reasserted himself. *We must feed.*

Not here, wailed Cormac, horrified at the idea of corrupting this place.

No, not in this village. People are accounted for.

Rory did not often feel the need to nourish that part of himself, and he wondered at Eamon's insatiability. He'd experienced exactly how his father, and grandfather as well, had gorged themselves on other's lives, and it sickened him. There was no need. It was repulsive, a sin if you believed such things, and he resisted.

But the resulting headache that rolled through his brain like thunder was not going away, and so Rory drove to Dundalk, the first city of any size on the route back to Dublin, driving faster than the speed limit and unconcerned about the Garda or anything else. Eamon kept hammering within his mind, demanding. Rory would have to hunt. It was not like at Knockaulin House, where loyal retainers had willingly allowed a sip here and there, such donations returned in the form of extended life. Nor was it like those times when the Kavanaghs had dealt with the unruly or the dangerous, emptying them of their life force before their bodies were disposed of by deputies and others dependent on the family.

They came into Dundalk, a flat, industrial city of red brick and sooty stone, spread out along a river flowing to the bay. Quays and warehouses and pubs of the docklands offered plenty of opportunities.

A sex worker of indeterminate gender approached Rory as he strolled along the sidewalk in the blowing mist. "Now, you're a fine lad," as their arm slipped into Rory's and they turned off from the street into an alley. "What would be your pleasure?"

And it was pleasure. As the sex worker leaned in for a kiss, Rory began the process and for the first time understood Eamon's cravings. The intoxicating intensity of this person's essence, neither male nor female but something between, even above, touched him in a way that other encounters had not. Those had been strictly limited transactions (except for the one in Dublin). This was something more.

Now you see. Some are different. Eamon shared his memory of Marco's life force, and of Darrick's until that connection was rudely severed. It made Rory's head spin as though he'd chugged back a bottle of bourbon.

Eamon was draining the sex worker rapidly, energy pulsing bright between Rory's body and the one slowly sagging in his embrace. Even as Rory felt the collective less than wholly satisfied, he forced himself away, set himself against his lineage to let this youth live. Cormac joined him, and between them they made Eamon release.

The connection broke. He pulled away from the transgender youth, so that his body slid down the wall. He shook himself, looked around, saw nothing in the dimness but walls with windows bricked in, leaking trash bins, a loading dock at the blank end. The youth was unconscious, but breathing. He dragged their inert form to the dock and laid them gently on the concrete. They looked so helpless, but nothing could be done about that. Rory took off his jacket and tucked it around the youth's torso. At least they'd not be soaked through if the rain thickened.

Rory felt as though a vise had been removed from his head. His interior committee was quieted, sated with new energy. But later that night, at the hotel in Dublin, Cormac reached out again, seeking Rory in the small space he'd carved out for himself and that Rory allowed only his uncle to know about.

Eamon is damaged.

"I know."

How much longer do you think we can contain him?

Rory had no answer.

Even if we could, it would be like this forever.

"Forever. Locked in with a madman." Even as Rory responded, he clenched at the thought of his father finding them, overhearing their plot. "But what can we do?"

If you can find a way to free yourself, even if it means our death, you must.

"How is that possible?"

Long silence. Finally Cormac spoke. *When the battle comes with Darrick, we help him win.*

Rory felt fear, now, but also a deeper bond with his uncle.
"Will Darrick destroy us?"
No answer.

Chapter 20

They were walking back from dinner when she saw a Garda car moving slowly through the village. Lourana pulled Darrick into a side street and then the shelter of a store's back doorway.

"What?"

"Look."

They peeked around the corner. The brightly marked car was driven by a policewoman, and the male passenger was examining the sidewalks and businesses left and right as they crept through Killeshandra.

No doubt in her mind who they were looking for, nor in Darrick's either when his eyes met hers.

They slipped through the back door of a pub and found a dark booth. Not that this was any concealment, but it was better than being on the street, visible enough she supposed as Americans even without a description of them. Which the police surely had. They hunched over their drinks, tea for Darrick and a Jack-and-Coke for her, and watched the doors like desperadoes. After an hour, they took a circuitous route back to the farmhouse, collected their things, and were gone as if they'd never been there.

They headed west, with no more idea of their destination than that B&B owner's few words about Donegal, wild and unvisited. As he drove, she reached out and took his hand, sorry for the distance between them, ashamed of her doubts. He gave her a flash of a smile, but the mood was grim and they spoke little until they'd been on the road an hour.

"Maybe we should ditch the car," she offered.

"It has to go back to the airport."

God, he can be so legalistic, she thought.

"We could turn it in somewhere, get a new one."

"If they know about this one, I don't think that will help for very long."

"Then let's leave it at the other airport, what is it, Shannon? And fly out."

"Where to?"

And that, of course, was the question. No refuge in West Virginia, or anywhere.

They let the silence fill the car and didn't try to break it again. Nothing to be said. He withdrew his hand from hers to put it on the steering wheel. He was as knotted up with concentration as though he were driving through a wall of fog.

They pulled into an Applegreen store and brought some food, sausage and potatoes in foil-lined bags, the familiarity of Coke in its red can. The highway was busy and the store lot full of coming and going, so they drove on. A sign led them off the highway to a side road, and a pull-off at the historic site that might allow for two or maybe three cars.

A gigantic boulder loomed over them, propped on two others, its flat top surmounted by a white cross.

"What on earth?"

Darrick got out and stood staring at the boulder. She came up behind him but he didn't move or turn. She was ready to shake him when he moved forward to follow a little track that went up one side of the rock. He disappeared for a moment and then appeared, standing on the top, next to the cross. He looked down at her, and maybe it was just the angle but he looked so sad.

"It's a Mass rock," he said. "I've been reading, how when the English ruled Ireland they outlawed Catholic worship. People met with outlaw priests at landmarks like this to celebrate Mass. They did this so faithfully that those paths are still visible."

Lourana clambered up to join him. From the top, you could see the trail those faithful had walked extended across the landscape, a narrow way that threaded through a tumble of stones and disappeared toward a single church spire marking a village.

"You know, when I was a kid I went to Mass, as required. I said my confession, did the proper rituals. I believed, but gradually it became something that I had to do. I didn't feel any more holy when I came out of the church with my sins forgiven than when I went in. But this . . ."

It gave her a weird feeling to be standing on top of a church. Her people had never held much with religion — she didn't have strong feelings for it or against it, but still.

"I know it's a fool's errand to think that somehow, magically, I'm going to learn something about my past just from being on the ground in Ireland. The museum exhibits, the castles, I've enjoyed it all, but nothing has really connected with me until this place, seeing the layers of the past here."

Lourana couldn't offer any comfort, thought she heard the utter loneliness in his words. She touched his arm and went down but when she looked back he was still on the rock, and she thought probably that's how it used to be, people gathered on the ground and the priest up there. Closer to God. Finally Darrick started down and she felt relieved, though she couldn't have said why.

"This probably marked a Neolithic grave, what's left of a dolmen or something," Darrick said as they got into the car. "I think about that, the fear and awe that drove people to raise these stones, long ago, for a ruler or a god. And then thousands of years later, a faith that set people walking for miles, in hazard of their lives, to celebrate Mass at a pagan table."

They unwrapped their lunches and ate in silence. The shadow of the rock moved across the hood of the car.

"Do we fight or keep running? For how long? The money is running out, even if I did have back pay for vacations never taken. I have to work. We have to live. We have to eat," he said, waving his fast-food lunch. "We can't run forever."

"So, what then?"

"I'll have to confront Rory. Them. The Kavanaghs."

"Can you?"

"I don't know. I wish I could believe like this," and he looked up at the cross. "That God is on our side, that we'll escape again. But I'm afraid. I think they're more powerful now, with another generation."

"Eamon isn't like he was, right? Sometimes he seems to be almost babbling."

Darrick pushed at his glasses. "Maybe. But there's Rory, too. And being here might be different for them. They might get something from the land, some strength, that I surely am not. They're kings, after all."

Lourana scoffed at that. "Just because they believe it don't make it so." But she remembered seeing the genealogy, carefully linked from recent times through history back to legend. At least some of it must be true. The Kavanaghs had genuine connections to the land, and she felt that herself back in West Virginia.

Darrick had unfolded the tourist map. "Donegal, she said?"

She bent closer and looked at the northwest corner of the map, a jagged coast, small dots that indicated villages that she knew now were nothing of any size, and bare space. That was Donegal. "It looks pretty empty."

"Maybe that's not so good. We'd stand out."

"What about Galway?" Her finger traced a line down, past Sligo (*why do I know that name? Oh, the Yeats exhibit*) and then to the city on a long bay that indented the coast. Her mother used to sing a song about watching the sun go down on Galway Bay.

Darrick didn't respond. He'd gone deep inside himself.

"Darrick," she said gently, "what about Galway?"

He seemed to refocus, with his finger traced highways down from where they'd stopped, but said nothing.

She thought of her little cottage, perched on the mountainside above Redbird, and those snowbound days when they became friends and lovers before the horrors bonded them together in a whole different way. She thought nothing could come between them, after that, but she used to think that about Steve as well.

They drove in silence, for the most part, before stopping at a pub overlooking the water. A band was playing inside and Lourana caught his quick, embarrassed glance at her, then he went back to the mechanics of parking.

The place was crowded but they were directed back to a two-top in an alcove away from the stage. The waitress was brisk, menu-drinks-orders, flashing a quick grin when Darrick asked if the mussels came from nearby.

"Wouldn't it be my own brother who works the mussel farm up on Killary Fjord," she said, nodding toward the water gleaming in the setting sun. "You could get no fresher unless you gather them yourself."

Mussels. Lourana didn't feel that adventurous, not with fish and chips on the menu.

The alcove had two other tables, one empty, one with a man and woman bent over their dinners. They made an odd pair. She was a mousy little thing, with old-fashioned glasses and flat ashy hair. He was big-shouldered, with greasy black hair falling over his forehead beneath a stained fisherman's cap.

"Oh go on." The man didn't bother to keep his voice down.

"I remember that, well enough." She ducked her head as she spoke.

He looked up, a bone in one hand, his dark eyes piercing as he glared at her. "Sure maybe he was right."

Hostility radiated from them. Lourana couldn't tell if they were husband and wife, brother and sister, or maybe people who'd worked together so long that they had sort of grown together in an ugly way.

"But then again . . ." with another head-duck.

"And perhaps he was talking through his arse." This was louder yet, loud enough that even with the band, people turned. The woman shrank away as though he'd strike her with the bone he still held.

Lourana saw the man flinch. His thick eyebrows went up, his eyes went wide, and he stood with a screech of chair legs. The man tossed the bone on his plate and stumbled away, the woman following as though led on a string as he shoved a path through the crowd.

"Darrick," she said, low.

"I'm sorry."

"I thought you wouldn't do that."

"I couldn't help it." He looked at her now and she could see how rattled he was, maybe almost as much as she was. "Just until we had some distance."

Their food arrived with a flourish and another grin for the tourists, but Lourana saw the waiter consider the half-finished pints at the empty table.

Still, she was hungry, and the fish was sizzling from the fryer and smelled fantastic, and Lourana could almost hear her grandmother saying that starvation wasn't going to fix any of your problems anyhow so you might as well eat up.

Darrick had a bowl full of shiny black shells. So those were mussels. He searched into the shells with a little fork, extracting the orange animals one by one. The clatter of tines and rustle of empties discarded into a bucket made up all their conversation. It wasn't until they were walking to the car that Darrick said, "Such terrible rage. How do they go on?" He shook his head.

And she wondered, *How do we go on?*

Chapter 21

The call came in early enough, too early for most but Rory had been restless and already been out for a run. He almost didn't pick up, but Eamon clamored, *That's the druid, that's him.*

"It's time we had a chat."

"You have news for us — for me?"

"Yes, and something you should see."

He told Rory they'd meet at a place called the Shannon Pot, along the Blacklion to Glangevlin Road. It was marked with brown tourist signs. "Oh, and you should be wearing wellies, it's a mite mucky there."

As he'd promised, the place wasn't hard to find. A long flat-topped ridge marked the skyline. From the parking lot, a gate opened onto a path through tussocky fields with sheep grazing. Rory recognized violets and buttercups, familiar enough from home.

Cathbad arrived in a small white car, wearing baggy khakis and a tight vest over a too-big shirt, looking not at all druid-like.

As they moved down the path, Rory noticed the yellow flowers and Cathbad caught the direction of his glance.

"Those are primroses, or cowslips. In Gaelic, *sabhaircín*. Tastes like lettuce." He bent and plucked a leaf and put it in his mouth, chewed and swallowed, but lingered on the path. "Year by year they advance their blooming. As do most all the flowers. The swallow and swift return for the insects, their migrations timed to the sun's clock, but things are out of kilter."

He shook his head and moved on, following the path toward a cluster of trees.

Rory had never taken much notice of plants, except when vines caught his feet or briers slashed him on a run. Yet here he was contemplating flowers in an Irish bog. He felt Cormac whispering at the edge of his awareness.

You are beginning to see.

Are you doing this?

You share what draws my attention.

Eamon broke in. *Better our attention on Darrick.* Rory stumbled, his father's bitter rage and skewed senses overcoming him. He reached out for a branch and got a handful of sharp thorns. All the other awarenesses retreated as he shook blood from his fingers.

"The worse for you that the pool is not shaded by hazel but by blackthorn. Keeper of dark secrets," said Cathbad.

"Keeper of damned thorns," Rory muttered. The small white flowers had concealed the long spikes.

"It's a chieftain tree so I'd not be cursing it."

Rory thought the druid seemed to be aware of sacredness everywhere, or maybe just pretended to be as part of his act.

The pool itself was nearly circular, black water overhung by blooming trees. There was not a breath of wind but the surface rippled and shuddered like the back of a horse bothered by flies.

"How deep is this?"

The druid was staring at the water. "It used to be said it was bottomless, but divers went down and found a bottom at 50 feet. A strong current runs into a crack in the earth. In any accounting, it's very deep, and extremely cold. This is a land of underground passages. Nearby are marble caves, and waters disappear and spring forth all across the landscape."

"Why are we here?" Rory was growing tired of the man's atmospherics, how he might as well have been wearing a pointed wizard hat and carrying a staff to go with the cryptic announcements and deep tone.

"Its name is *Lag na Sionna*, the hollow of the Shannon, the source of Ireland's great river," he went on, heedless as a professor before a class of nodding students. "There are two legends about its beginnings. In one, the granddaughter of the sea god came here to pluck forbidden fruit from the Tree of Knowledge. When she ate, the pool rose up and took her. In the other, she came looking for the Salmon of Wisdom, and the salmon drew her down into the pool that spread out over the land."

Eamon was stirring now. And Padraig, and Domnall.

"All very nice," Rory grated, struggling to maintain control. "But what has that to do with the bigger question?"

"This has long been a votive site. People threw in weapons, even gold. Do you have anything to give?"

"So you expect me to, what, throw in my watch?" Rory shook his wrist and the metal band slithered against his skin. He'd left his sleek Apple Watch in the room, felt compelled to wear this heavy piece of industrial timekeeping, his father's Rolex. He wouldn't at all mind making the sacrifice.

"No, something more important. The whole truth of your quest."

"I'm looking for the connections to my family, the ancient Kavanagh line of kings. We have the genealogy to prove that." Rory saw the family tree branching out from Adam, a document as spurious as those once drawn for other potentates. "We left Ireland to establish ourselves in America, and thrived, but feel cut off from our heritage."

"Millions come home to find those very answers. Ireland's children are like the seeds of dandelion, scattered far on the breezes." Cathbad's shrewd eyes gleamed deep within the fleshy folds. "But I feel there's more to your story. Layers. Depths beyond depths, like this pool."

Rory squatted down in the damp grass by the water's edge. The pool was as black at close hand as it was from a distance. Like coal, it gathered all the light of sky and sun into itself. He plucked a primrose flower and tossed it on the water, where it floated and moved with the invisible current.

"Not an unworthy offering," said Cathbad. "The plant is considered sacred. Or was, once upon a time. As kings were. That you have preserved your crest through emigration and struggles is a testament to the persistence of your royal blood. The legacy that has carried through all your generations, father to son."

The druid seemed to know and not know. *Like a carnival psychic, he draws the answers from you while he picks your pocket,* complained Patrick.

More, there's more. Eamon. *He was put in our path for a reason.*

Rory stood and moved back, before Eamon's flailing could unsteady him and sent him pitching into the cold water. A wise move, because his father suddenly muscled forward, taking control of Rory both body and voice.

"We must have revenge." Rory could not stop the rumbling voice that could sometimes manage only disconnected phrases. Eamon was not to be checked. "MacBrehon. He killed me. Us."

The druid watched dispassionately as Rory struggled.

"Fist in my brain. He has power."

Rory felt his throat clenching almost until he could not breathe. Maybe Eamon would throttle him at last, as he sometimes had threatened when Rory was a child.

"There's more than one Kavanagh banging about that noggin of yours."

Rory stared at him, helpless to respond.

"Let Rory speak with me."

Eamon must have responded the authority in that voice, because the spasm passed. Rory took a deep, shuddering breath, as though he'd been held underwater and allowed to surface.

"I don't understand everything that happened. My father was attacked by this Darrick MacBrehon, inside our home, and mortally wounded."

"And what precipitated that?"

"The man had himself been attacked, I believe by one of our associates. He's got a kind of power to respond to strong negative emotion by forcing it back, and he can kill, that we know. What we don't know is where it came from." Rory breathed deep, should he be submerged again. "My father demands vengeance."

"Your father. And some others, I'd be thinking."

"My father Eamon."

"Who is the strongest."

Rory nodded. "And his brother, my uncle, Cormac. And their father Patrick. His father Domnall, and Padraig who came from Ireland first."

"That's quite a crowd. Tell me about this possession."

Cormac, suddenly, was in his throat. "We are inheritors of a great power, or a great curse. I am Cormac, not intended to exist, there being only one Kavanagh in each generation to wield this power."

"And that would be?" The druid seemed unfazed by the silky new voice, the presence of another ghost spilling from Rory's mouth.

"They, we actually, have the ability to draw on a person's life force and make it our own. We can sip, if we choose, and do no harm, even share some of our potency with our donors. Or we can take the entire life."

Cathbad raised an eyebrow at that.

"Not all of us are killers," Rory said, regaining himself. "Cormac and I. We've never willingly taken a life. I didn't know the whole of it until I stood at my father's bedside as he was dying. We don't want this power."

"Yet you've inherited it."

"My father took Cormac's life. And his father's."

Eamon was there, stronger than before. "We must pass the gift before death. My father's life was mine just as he took his father's."

"And Cormac?"

"Should not have been."

Rory felt as though he'd run a marathon in the desert. His body and mind were depleted. Eamon taunted him, *perhaps a sip from this druid.*

If I was Cathbad, I'd be walking away from this, Rory thought.

"I must say, I've never encountered such a being, not in real life nor yet in the old tales. You're not of the Fair Folk, not even the solitary powers like the banshee or the pooka. Closest, perhaps, to the lean-nán sidhe who battens on the lives of poets. Something else going on here, something even more ancient, perhaps." Cathbad looked up at the long ridge. "They say the water of the Shannon starts up on those tops, makes it way to this black pool, but no one's ever see that water flowing. Doesn't mean it's not there."

A car pulled into the lot and two young women began to take the path toward them, to the Shannon Pot. One of them laughed and tossed back her long hair.

"Time we were going," Cathbad announced. "I will think on all this. Meantime, rest easy until I call you. I have methods to locate this Darrick."

All the Kavanaghs were startled, a ripple within like that on the black water.

"How?"

Cathbad made a gesture, offered a hint of a smile.

Rory was silent as the tumult took hold within.

Is he truthful? What are his powers? Psychic? Fraud? A druid indeed?

We could compel the truth, said Domnall, asserting himself over the others. Domnall who had been called Old Scratch like the devil, and who gave rise to the miners' legend that the Kavanaghs could "strip a man to the bones."

But Eamon, for once, was reluctant. *Can't risk.*

"Can you take us to him?" Rory voiced, for all within.

"Wait for my call. We will return to Dún Ailinne when the time is right. But before that, you must ready yourselves to deal with the son of the brehon."

Eamon exulted, *Kill Darrick with the druid's help.*

In his space apart, Rory thought the druid offered nothing of the sort.

We will stand on the hill.

But to what point, Rory returned. Just to verify our claims?

Not confirmation. Eamon struggled to express his ideas. *We will regain our ancestors. All the others. Before Padraig. Their power.*

Rory quailed at this news, the thought of an endless line of Kavanaghs crowding his body and mind.

Cormac was a calming presence, behind and apart from his father. He spoke to Rory in that hidden place they now shared. *We will not let him win.*

Chapter 22

Rory was waiting.

For Dreama to call. For the druid's next summons. For a way out of the future revealed by Eamon, a tide of ancestors rising out of the depths like a tsunami.

Cormac whispered, *I'm with you.*

Rory thought bitterly that he had no choice, about Cormac or the others. He was a servant to the ravenous dead.

The sky outside the Galway hotel room was black as the Shannon Pot. Lights around the bay reflected in the water, but there wasn't a star in the sky. He kept seeing that pool invisibly filled, invisibly emptying into the earth, ripples on the water, flowers floating, his left hand bloodied. The thorns had driven a poison into the wounds and his fingers were swollen and aching.

The druid had promised he would be in touch very soon, an appointment that Rory must keep, but he gave no other information. He wondered again if Cathbad actually had some kind of arcane powers or if he was just a sleight-of-hand artist, a song-and-dance man fleecing the gullible. It was too much to hope that he might be freed from his ancestors through anything connected to that glib man.

Eamon had driven him again last night to feed, and to leave another husk where a life had once been. He tried not to look into the face of the victim as Eamon and the others used his body to sate them all, but it was his hands that touched, and held, then bundled the corpse down a bank into a weed-choked demolition site.

I'm a criminal, he thought, long and short of it. The elders might have been able to rely on retainers for sustenance but out in the world, it's different. They've made me a hunter. A serial killer, to put no gloss on reality. His father's hunger drove him, his grandfather's and that of the others.

Rory could scarcely remember the man he'd been before his father's felling. He was beginning to feel the way each of their personalities was taking root in his mind, like Cormac's sensuality, and pushing him into actions that frightened or sickened him. Eamon's impatience. His grandfather's businesslike counsel. Domnall's rapacity. Padraig's brutality. And something, something beyond. The other ancestors? It was all dark, so dark. Would they eventually be all there was of Rory?

He was saved from a deeper plunge by the chirping of his iPhone, and Dreama's face on the screen.

"Hello Dreama."

"Hello my love!" She was in a lacy nightgown, emerald green, and he knew she'd carefully chosen it for this call.

"Good to see you."

"I wish you were seeing me from closer up." She dropped one strap, looked at him through the fringes of her black hair.

Rory was aroused, immediately, his cock rising against the sweatpants he'd slipped on after a shower. He flushed, embarrassed, and Cormac was whispering an apology, but his uncle's desire continued to flood Rory's mind and body.

"Are you okay? Not working too hard?" She morphed from seductress to nurse, just that quickly, and Rory was relieved at the shift.

"It's quite the schedule at this meeting."

"Slip out the back door and go see some of the world."

Cormac was insistent, *please*, and Rory stopped trying to control his uncle. He let his voice and mannerisms come through.

"I want you. I want to taste you. I want to watch how your face relaxes as you fall into sleep."

Dreama sighed.

Rory could step back and watch their romance, a somewhat interested third party. Cormac's love was almost as strong as Eamon's rage, but Rory was stirred by this beautiful woman as well. Or maybe that, too, was only Cormac: Though he'd had brief relationships enough in college, they'd never approached this intensity. Never been allowed to.

For a moment, he saw the face of the sex worker as he laid them down in the wet alleyway. His erection reasserted itself. I've never been attracted to guys, he thought, but then he wasn't sure what that Bowie-esque figure represented, male or female, something resonating between, and his spirit — it was a man, after all, physically — so intense. He remembered how their spiky hair was tipped with rain. How their crimsoned lips had parted. Those lips merged with Dreama's until her voice summoned him back.

"It's strange you are in Ireland," Dreama was saying. "My mother is there, too."

She stopped as though she wished she'd not brought up Lourana.

"I thought it was odd you didn't know where she was," Rory said, fully reclaiming himself.

"She's gotten odd. Very odd."

"Understandable."

"Secretive. Even with me. I don't know why she's running around the world with this Darrick, but I wish she'd calm down and come home."

Rory nodded agreement. Dreama didn't realize she'd betrayed her mother. Not that it mattered now, of course, except that it bound the two of them even closer.

Chapter 23

"I wish I'd never let you inside that night."

Lourana heard the words come boiling out of her mouth and there was no taking them back.

Darrick had been looking out the window, avoiding her anger as he would do, always, because it was painful to him, but there was something about his stony back that just got under her skin. They were bickering about what to watch on television, something that petty, because the big issues couldn't be debated or solved. And then he'd just gotten up and gone to the window, where dusk was spreading into the room. She waited for him to answer, to turn around, to work out this knot they were in. But nothing.

That got her ire up. She almost spat the words, wanting to suck them back even as they'd come out, hot as rivets.

"I wish you hadn't either," he said, without turning around. "I dragged you into this horror that I didn't understand. Still don't."

"I'm sorry. I didn't mean that." She wanted to crawl under the bed, under the hotel, bury her shame.

"Of course you did. Right then."

Darrick turned. Even from here, she could see that his eyes were shiny with tears.

"I'm just so damn frustrated," she said.

"Me too."

"I'm so sorry. You know I love you."

She waited for the response. *I know he loves me, why won't he say it?* But Darrick went back to staring out the window without a word.

They managed a perfunctory kiss at bedtime. A placeholder for when they were able to get past this. *You never learnt to bite your tongue, Mama used to say. You just gotta say whatever comes through your head no matter what the consequences. It ain't plain speaking, Lourana, it's just hurtful.*

The morning after, things were just as raw. They ate breakfast, or at least some of it, in the fusty little dining room, then prepared for the day.

Back in the room, he laid out their situation quietly and precisely. There was no point in changing their flight to leave early. No point in evasion. They'd travel back to Dublin the end of next week and go home, as planned. The Kavanaghs had the resources to pursue them, and it appeared they would, until they came to some kind of confrontation. Whatever awaited them, here or there, the location wouldn't matter.

Lourana only nodded. It was the same non-answer they'd known all along. What did they have to do anyway, other than sit in a room and stew? Get into another fight?

"My affairs are in order," he said. "You'll inherit what I have. The contact information for my lawyer is in my wallet. There's a copy of my will in my files."

Lourana swallowed hard. Next of kin. Disposal of body, if there was one. "You have Dreama's number."

Because I have kin. Someone to notify.

"Well, that's that. We might as go on pretending we're tourists for a little while." And he began setting out the day in his methodical, civil-servant way.

Lourana felt cold and wished he would get his nose out of that damned map and take her in his arms. She could go to him, but couldn't bring herself to make that step, just watched as he went on circling the sites. Cathedrals, the Latin Quarter, something called the Claddagh. Start here, then go there. *As though organization could save us.*

They drove in to Galway's city center and parked at a lot on Market Street. No rain was forecast til evening.

"Let's try to have a good time," he said.

"You're right." She smiled, though she was thinking *the prisoner enjoyed a hearty meal before death.*

Galway had church spires and gray ancient buildings and water everywhere, river and canal and the glittering bay and the ocean beyond. Lourana never got tired of looking at water, whether that bog they'd crossed with flowers blooming on the water, or slow streams with swans like something out of a fairy tale, or rushing rivers with fishermen casting from the middle. She wondered if any of the rivers of Ireland flowed red with acid like those she knew back home. But they didn't have coal here. It was peat instead, that they burned in fireplaces. Or used to do so — maybe that was all in the romantic past.

They were camouflaged in the crowd, just two more faces among the throngs visiting Eyre Square and staring at the Lynch Castle, a gray cube unremarkable except that a father had hanged his own son from that very window for murder, so the name became notorious. A small museum or gallery was promoting an exhibit on "Brighid in Myth and History" that looked interesting, but they didn't stay long. A professor or something was speaking to a packed room, mostly a solemn tour group of young Asian men, maybe college students.

They bypassed the Galway City Museum, closed on Mondays, and visited the Spanish Arch. Even as they looked at this, and looked at that, their eyes snagged on every red-haired man in the street.

They crossed the Corrib River. Lourana looked over the side at the waters thrashing below. It was a powerful river, like those that came down from the mountains in West Virginia. People had tied colored ribbons to the metal railing. They flailed in the wind. She wondered if they marked death, or love, or a child's birth. Then they were in the section called The Claddagh. Flat-faced, many-windowed buildings had been painted in various colors, some bright as a child's toy. Boats were tied up along the pier, others pulled up onto the shore. An old wooden boat, a rowboat but fashioned prettier than the flat-bottomed one kids used to paddle around a neighbor's pond, was rotting into the ground. Grass grew up through its ribs.

Next to another old church was a garden and a statue of the Madonna in a rock-built enclosure.

"What is that?" she whispered.

"A grotto," he answered. "It's a shrine to Mary."

She'd seen similar but smaller niches for such built into the front of cobbled houses in Redbird, placed there by the immigrant stonemasons who'd built walls and bridges and mined coal as well. This was a whole lot more. Darrick went in the gate and they followed the pathways through the rose garden, thorny branches not yet blooming. He stood in front of the statue, motionless. She wondered if he was praying. If nothing else about Ireland had caught his attention, this had — this and the Mass rock. He turned abruptly and caught her watching, then gave a little half-smile as if to say, how quaint, all this superstition is behind me.

Lunch in a boisterous pub did not allow for conversation, though there had been little enough before. Lourana knew her own thoughts circled endlessly, and his did likewise she was sure. They ate, hunched close to their food at a tiny table where the pot of tea took took up too much space.

"One thing about Ireland," she said.

He bent his head toward her.

"You've got tea anytime, anywhere."

Darrick laughed at that and raised his cup. She felt the ice begin to melt.

It was good feel like a couple again. She let her hand find Darrick's as they walked, and he squeezed it like he'd never let it go.

At one point earlier in the day, they'd passed a granite pillar with the image of two hands clasping a heart, with a crown above. It was a symbol they'd seen over and over again, on signs and even printed on the map Darrick clutched. The Claddagh ring, named for the fishing village. A store had a large poster about it in the window, and Darrick, who seemed to have an endless appetite for history, stopped and read it carefully. Lourana scanned the text, the heart representing love, the crown for loyalty, the hands for friendship. Produced in Galway since 1700 or before. Then a lot of details about the makers, including one who'd supposedly learned to be a goldsmith while enslaved by the Moors.

Darrick started inside, turned to look for her, and she followed.

The small shop was bursting with Claddagh symbols, on everything from rings and necklaces to linens, glassware, even jeweled dog leashes.

"Good evening to you," said a young woman behind the jewelry counter, "and welcome to Claddagh House."

Lourana saw her eyes flick toward their left hands.

"Perhaps you'd like to look at our rings. There's none finer in Galway." She pulled out a tray of rings with some of the hearts set with stones, others entirely gold. "Ruby for true heart, emerald for our Emerald Isle."

Darrick picked one out, one with a green stone. "They're beautiful," he said.

Lourana was thinking, *and pricey.*

"I think this will fit," Darrick said, and lifted her hand.

Her heart tumbled.

Darrick turned the ring in his fingers, looked at her, then slipped it on her ring finger. The heart was pointing toward her.

"Perfect," said the shopkeeper. "He has quite the eye for sizing."

"Darrick . . ."

"There's a long tradition in how you wear the ring," the woman went on. "If it's on the left ring finger with the heart pointing at the fingertips, then the wearer is engaged. If the heart points toward the wrist, then married."

"Will you take this ring, Lourana?" He was solemn, wide-eyed.

"Yes," she said, "but that don't mean all the way."

The shopkeeper's mouth pursed and she busied herself with putting away the tray, looking everywhere but at Lourana.

She pulled the ring off and turned it around. "Not yet, anyway." It would have been easy to just go along, but something in her pulled back violently.

Darrick looked away and she saw his hand tremble before he stuck it in the pocket of his windbreaker.

I faced death with him. Flew around the world with him. Why can't I let go now? She argued with herself as he paid and they went out into the evening made darker by the gathering clouds.

"Please wear it, Lourana. Keep it turned that way until you can say yes with your whole heart."

She touched the ring, wondered if she would move it to her right hand, the one that meant no commitment, but that would break him.

Now she wished she'd just shut up when he put the ring on her finger. *What would it have cost you?*

They moved on in silence. The charming sites seemed leaden now. It would rain soon but they were not far from where they'd parked. As they passed the Brighid show, still open, that same professor stepped from the doorway and handed them a pamphlet.

"You'll be wanting to see this installation, I expect."

Brilliant art filled the room behind him, paintings and stained glass pulsing with light.

"Brighid is the great healer," he said. "Come, have a look."

"Is he the owner?" she whispered.

"Maybe a docent or something."

They went in. Why not, after all?

All around the room were images of a woman with trees and swans, the sun and the moon. Flames. In one, she lifted her cloak and hung it on a sunbeam. Lourana noticed that unlike earlier, there were only two or three people drifting around the place.

"You've seen these, surely." The man with the twinkling eyes of a leprechaun showed them a cross made out of dried grass. "This is Brighid's cross. As she watched by the bedside of a dying chieftain, she picked up rushes from the floor and wove a cross. Of course, it also represents the four quarters of the year, because she was a goddess in Ireland long before the priests arrived."

They walked around the gallery as he spun out tales of "Ireland's second-most-favorite saint."

"Her name means power or virtue, or exalted one. She has her holy wells and churches all over the island, but Kildare is her center, where the fire temple can still be seen that her women tended in pre-Christian times."

Brighid might be runner-up to St. Patrick for popularity, but it's obvious this man thought she was number one. A fire temple — that sounded interesting. Lourana tried to see the gold-colored medallion that showed under his vest as he pointed out more symbols on the art work. She glanced at Darrick but he was distant, shut down.

"It's recorded that she turned a wooden column into a living tree with one touch," he continued.

"It's getting late. I'm tired," Darrick whispered.

She looked out to the dark streets and wondered if this city was safe, being a port and all, but the man at the hotel had reassured her, "Oh, it's safe as houses, sure enough. Even the rough parts are not so bad, unless you get around the young men drinking cans after midnight. Behind the railway station and such."

The man caught their exchange. "Time to go home? I'll walk with you as I'd be going up to the car park myself."

And just like that, he attached himself. Lourana was reminded of the fat boy in middle school who'd tried so hard to make friends, who'd join up with any group until it, too, turned on him. She'd been no better than the rest, ducking his frantic efforts to connect.

"You really must stop in to the Church of St. Nicholas," he chattered as they left the gallery. "Columbus worshipped there, it's well documented, before he embarked for the New World."

"You did want to see that, right?" she whispered, remembering the circled sites. Darrick looked out of it, just tired probably, but he nodded yes.

"For just a minute."

"I've not introduced myself. My name is Cathbad, properly said Kaava in Gaelic." The man bent forward in a sort of bow.

"I'm Lou — " she paused, sensing Darrick stiffen next to her. "And Rick."

"So pleased to meet you. I'm a scholar of ancient history so you'll excuse my rambling on about things. And here we are."

Though the church was lit up for visitors, it was empty when they went in.

"This is the largest medieval parish church still in continuous use, here in Ireland. Parts of it date from the 14th century, but there are ruins beneath, Christian and pre-Christian."

Lourana tried to tote up the years, more than 500, not counting whatever had stood here before. And that was nothing compared to Brighid, who went back to, maybe Stonehenge. It was hard to get her mind around how old everything was.

The church itself was like too many she'd seen already. Tall and hollow, sounds echoing. Stained glass. Chairs lined up in rows instead of pews. The vaulted ceiling, however, was painted royal blue and gold. Really pretty, and it reminded her of home and the WVU colors. Paintings hung here and there showing a severe-looking man with a short beard. If that was St. Nicholas, he was nothing like the Santa Claus she knew.

Cathbad was showing Darrick a headless statue and talking about Cromwell. Lourana wandered, looking at a plaque, a square block of a tomb, til she found a baptismal font with a dog carved on it, which seemed like an odd thing to choose. She kept hoping Darrick would call it quits in that abrupt way he had, give the man a polite but final thank you, and they could head for the car.

She looked up to see Rory Kavanagh standing just to the side of the red doors.

"Darrick," she said, somewhere between a whisper and a cry.

He turned toward her, followed her gaze, and for a moment they were each frozen at the points of a triangle. Then the geometry broke down, and Rory and Darrick were moving toward each other. She watched as Cathbad inserted himself between them. Rory was talking, but it was all a jumble, the voices of Eamon and Cormac and others, like a radio between stations.

Darrick was not flinching. "I'll send you to hell," he said, as that golden band began to shimmer between them.

Rory shook his head, scrambled backward in panic, and then she saw him run for the nearest door.

"Come, my dear." Cathbad had hold of her arm. "Best not to get your curragh wedged between the breakers and the rocks."

Then they were outside, walking in the night, and she could see no shops open or anything but water, the river.

"Be calm, now, I mean you no harm."

"Darrick . . ."

Lourana felt herself being steered, and she looked back for the church but its silhouette was tangled with other buildings, or not where she thought it was. The strange man no longer seemed like a strange but innocuous acquaintance. She tested his grip but stayed silent, fearing a gun or a knife if she called out, but there seemed to be no one to hear.

"You'll be together again," he whispered.

Chapter 24

Rory had kicked around the city all day, too uncertain to do anything, run, work. Eating too much and drinking too much, feeling bloated, unsteady. Being played for a fool, he thought.

The druid said to stay close, be ready to respond quickly. "Be guided by me."

Wait on him. Eamon.

We must be ready. Cormac, but Rory knew his uncle's intentions did not mesh with Eamon's.

When the text came across with a cheery ding, Rory was only two streets from the church. It was a damp wait outside, shorter than it seemed, he was sure, but unpleasant enough that he was quick to respond to the second text. He opened the doors carefully.

Inside, the atmosphere was somewhere between a museum and a little-used library. Rory scanned the room, the unfamiliar furnishings and images (the Kavanaghs not being church people for as long as their memory extended) and spotted Cathbad and Darrick by one wall, Lourana standing alone. Everything was motionless as one of the painted icons, until Lourana saw him and said "Darrick."

Rory had no plan for what was to happen next. The druid had explained he would bring them together "for a parlay" but that they must be patient while he learned from Darrick's presence "what the nature of his power may be." Eamon was having none of that. He impelled Rory step by step toward his enemy, and now Darrick was moving toward him as well, swaying, his body unsure. Yet Rory felt the terror in his father's thoughts even as he lashed out, *the staggering fool.* Memories of crashing to the floor, drooling helplessness, the slow slide toward death.

The druid came between Rory and Darrick, talking low but urgently; Rory could barely hear him for the tumult in his head. "Keep your distance," he said, which alarmed Rory along with the concern he heard in Cathbad's voice. "Not the time."

Rory struggled to regain control of his body, awkwardly caught between Eamon's urging against his and Cormac's refusal. He came to a ragged halt.

Darrick had backed up a little. For all the insecurity in his gait, and despite his desk jockey appearance, Rory knew that the man was dangerous. Deadly. He remembered his own martial arts training, how a defensive posture was also offense, a block also a punch. Darrick seems to be always on the back foot but that was an illusion.

"I, we," Rory began, but his voice wouldn't obey him.

Avenge me! Eamon roared.

Rory tried again. "I don't wish . . ." but he was interrupted again, heard his grandfather's voice say *Listen,* and then Eamon was pushing past them all, reaching out through him, employing his body, his hands, trying to reach past the druid's outstretched arms, pull the life from Darrick and destroy him.

Darrick remained stock still. As Rory felt the connection made and the first flow of life begin to enter his body, he realized that Eamon's fanatical pursuit of Darrick was partly about family survival, but also about his hunger for that unusual energy.

Then a terrible pressure was exerted against him, like a gravitational force squeezing him from all sides at once.

"I'll send you to hell, Eamon, like I should have before."

Pain shot through his head as he felt his own throat form an incoherent, beastlike sound. He stumbled backward, turned, found the strength to get out of the church. Near the street, he bent double and vomited, his head aching as though he'd been struck by a car. He lowered himself to his hands and knees before he could fall.

Now you understand, his father said.

Rory felt a touch on his back, shuddered and crabbed away. When he turned to look, a shabby man was bending down to see his face. "Too much of a good thing," he chortled. "Oh the times I've touched my forelock to Galway's dirty cobbles, all for having a last pint."

Chapter 25

And then she was outside, she was in the shadow of the church, she was following a path by the river, and the man was holding her arm and guiding her to a car. He took her purse, her phone, and buckled her in. She felt both cosseted and restrained.

"Don't try to leap out or any such thing."

"So I'm your prisoner?"

"Do you feel yourself to be a prisoner?"

Oddly enough, she didn't. Not at all. Lourana blinked, tried to clear her head of whatever cobwebs had been spun there.

"You want to be with me. It will be in your best interest, and Darrick's."

He went around, got in, fussed with seat belt and lights. She watched him but felt no alarm as he started the car.

"Did you hypnotize me?"

"The traditional word is glamour," he said. "A bit of wizarding, if you will — the word meant enchantment, before it was reduced to mere elegance."

Enchantment? Lourana thought perhaps she was sleeping, dreaming, the scene in the church only a nightmare. But her common sense told her it had been no dream, and she was in a car with this leprechaun man going who knows where.

"Where is Darrick?"

No answer. The city was rapidly fading into countryside, dark except for a light at a farmhouse here or there, the glint of the emerging moon between clouds. She tried to watch for road signs, landmarks, but the few she saw quickly became confused. The car engine whined but otherwise, no sound. She matched silence for silence as she thought how she would escape, how she would find Darrick. And what to do about the Kavanaghs? For that, she had no plots or plans.

She was almost nodding off — *if I dream I'm falling asleep, will I wake up?* — when they turned off the road onto a track that continued deep into a forest. Trees pressed close on each side. A light appeared ahead. The track ended in a small clearing and a cottage with a light on beside the door.

He escorted her inside, indicated an armchair by the cold hearth. "Make yourself comfortable. I'll put the kettle on."

As he bustled about the kitchen, he introduced himself again. "I'm Cathbad, if you remember. I'm a teacher. And Forest Sage."

"What?"

"Leader of a grove, a group of believers. You would probably call me a druid."

"Druid?" She almost laughed, but realized he was serious, this strange man with the medallion swaying on its chain. "Did you conjure this up out of a cauldron?"

He looked a bit pained. "That's not what this is about, not it at all."

She watched him drop teabags into cups, open a package of cookies and scatter them on a plate. The kettle began to bubble.

"Milk, for you? Sugar?"

"Yes, please. Both."

An image of the Mad Hatter's tea party flashed, Alice sitting prim and proper as things got curiouser and curiouser.

She took the saucer and sipped the grassy-tasting tea, then wondered if that was such a good idea.

"Biscuit?"

She thought about the first night in Dublin, how Darrick had instructed her that cookies here were called biscuits. She remembered the first time making tea for Darrick in her own little house as the snowstorm raged, and couldn't stop tears from welling in her eyes.

"There's no shame in the weeping, now." His voice was soft, sympathetic. *He might be a psychopath.*

"How did you find us?"

"Members of my grove and allied groves. Like the trees, we're all around and completely invisible. A few pounds and but a moment to add a tracking device under your car. The GPS on my cell does the work." He ate a cookie in two bites.

"I don't believe you."

"You Americans think you've got it all over us for technology. Do you think I'm adept at only the mystic arts?" He grinned, his teeth small and to her mind, sort of like one of those lapdogs, a Pomeranian or Yorkie.

"Where is Darrick?" She said it so forcefully that the teacup rattled in the saucer, slopped over, and she set it down on a little knock-kneed table.

"He's well away from Rory Kavanagh, I can tell you that. Safe, for now, as you are. Be patient. Your best chance of cutting this Gordian knot lies with me."

Lourana glared at him. "You're helping them. The Kavanaghs."

"So you know there's more than one."

"I know them." Memories crowded her thoughts and she wondered if he could read her mind. "Why are you helping them?"

"I'm helping — neither side."

"But you are in touch with them."

"I am."

"And you know where Darrick is?"

"More or less. I haven't checked on his latest location."

"You brought us together at the church. Why would you do that?"

He looked at her intently and it seemed like she was revealed, to her shame. That he could see everything about her and Darrick, how she'd loved him so strongly and then bit by bit began to worry, and then to doubt, and then to pull back from the commitment that had been so secure. She flushed, remembering Darrick's face as he'd offered her the claddagh ring just a few hours ago. Lourana turned it on her finger. The heart still pointed away.

"I am truly sorry to have frightened you. I had to see for myself what these forces might be, if they existed at all. I've heard much from Rory, and those others within, about Darrick and you. But people can delude themselves."

"You could have killed us!"

"Possibly. Not likely. I couldn't know what I was dealing with until I saw it, and that demanded proximity." He seemed as unemotional about the situation as a robot.

"We aren't talking about a football game!"

"Definitely not. I have a lot of knowledge about the unseen forces in the world, and you must trust — "

"Hah!"

"Trust that I do not take this lightly. Wherever the Kavanaghs came by this power, it's like nothing I've ever encountered. Primeval. Remorseless as the very stones we stand on."

"They will kill."

"Have done. I know that. Perhaps we can find a solution less drastic."

"Than Darrick's death?"

"Or Rory's."

"He's a Kavanagh," she spat, the name a mouthful of filth.

The druid sipped from his cup and set it aside. "Rory is possessed by the past. You might think of him as a haunted house. I've seen something like this before, previous generations trying to reach through the living, but such incidents tend to be more about maintaining influence on the young, or gaining peace by completing some task. The Kavanaghs are well beyond that. I think young Rory would be happy indeed to be rid of his paters."

She thought about how she could hear her Pap and Mama, the older generations, the good advice they'd offered all life long. But it was just an echo in her memory, like music on repeat. Everyone carried family around in their heads that way. Except for Darrick.

"He, they, tried to kill us," she reminded Cathbad.

He nodded. "And you in turn tried to kill them."

"Darrick was protecting himself, protecting us. He doesn't attack people — he just pushes back."

"A defensive force, that I could see. An adamantine power."

"For good," she insisted. "Or not. Power is power. Much depends on the person who wields it. Even the most beneficent can find themselves acting otherthan their natures when put to the test."

"He responds to negative emotions. Hate or pride or lust."

"The seven deadlies," he said, getting up to go to the kitchen counter. "Add greed, sloth, gluttony, envy."

She could see the face of the newspaper editor, distorted with envy and lust, as he threatened his reporter Zadie Person and drove her away, then wrenched Lourana's shoulder to breaking and forced her to her knees. "That's the way I like to see a woman," he'd gloated, right before Darrick came in like a superhero and saved the day. Darrick had killed that man intentionally, unlike the ones who had threatened him before he realized what terrible power had come to him.

"More tea? It doesn't appear so."

"No thank you. Maybe you can conjure up some coffee." He smiled and flicked the button on the electric kettle to reheat.

"You know, the name Darrick is derived from the word for oak. Duir. Oak-hearted or strong. The same word is the source of druid."

As he prepared his tea, Lourana listened. Nothing. There was not a sound from the forest, no rumble of cars on a nearby highway.

"I need to use the restroom."

He indicated a door off the kitchen.

She really did have to go, but Lourana also wanted to scope out where she was. The tiny window in the bathroom wouldn't let a toddler escape. When she opened it and looked out, nothing but deep shadows and a sky with neither moon nor stars. The silence was barely broken by a soft sound that might be wind in the tree tops, or distant surf, so maybe they'd traveled along the coast. It felt weird not to have her phone, to be able to get an answer just that quick, see a dot on a map. She dried her hands on a stained and threadbare towel. Someone lived here. The druid? *I can't believe I'm using that word.* The soap bar was curled and cracked, so nobody had been around for a while, and the medicine cabinet was empty except for a thermometer and a bottle of paracetamol, whatever that was.

When she came out, she found him settled now in a kitchen chair, placed facing hers.

"I apologize for the state of the larder. No coffee to be found here. A glass of water?"

She shook her head.

"I'll provide the opening by sharing what I know of you. Your name is Lourana Taylor, from Redbird, West Virginia, and you were on a mission against the Kavanaghs long before Darrick appeared because the river had been killed with pollution from their mines. I'm correct?"

"Yes. Partly.

"What do you know about their powers?"

"You're the wizard."

He didn't react. She felt her anger dissipate. *More glamour?* Maybe. But if he was going to help Darrick, then she'd spill.

"You probably know all this from the Kavanaghs. Or at least their version of it. Anyway, they're what we call coal barons, in Appalachia. You had a feudal system, well, so do we. They own anything worth owning in Carbon County and all around, and what they don't own they control round the back way."

"But not just with money."

"Some of it's money, of course. Most mines are owned by corporations now, but the Kavanaghs are old-timey like. They keep their hands on the reins. The fire bosses and mine inspectors, they get paid off and fall in line like they're told. But fear's how they really rule. Have for generations."

His eyes really *were* strange, Lourana thought, small and set within folds of flesh, but intense, that light brown they call hazel.

"The miners used to say, and everyone else around town, that the Kavanaghs could strip a man to the bones. I thought it was just a turn of phrase — my own pap worked for them and he said they were a hard lot — but then I saw it with my own eyes, and felt it, too. They draw the life from you and you can watch it go, a golden light that passes from your body into theirs. They can stop or keep taking until they've sucked up every bit of life, all but the bones.

"I saw the beginning of that in the church. It was — appalling."

"It wasn't only the river they destroyed. My daughter had disappeared, like some other folks, and I was sure the Kavanaghs had a hand in that." She thought about finding Dreama, then, in that horrible crypt beneath the mansion where the Kavanaghs laid out the bones of their dead. How they had held each others' hands in the dark, waiting to be devoured as they'd seen done to Marco. His prolonged and torturous death under the hands of Eamon.

"Then Darrick showed up."

"He was just passing through and stopped for gas when he got crosswise of one of their creatures, who whacked him on the head and threw him down a mine crack on Kavanagh property. He survived, unlike the others he found down there. He got out and came to the door of the sweepstakes parlor where I was working. A real mess, bloodied up and smelling of rotting flesh, but said he'd come across a necklace down in that pit of bones and I thought it might be Dreama's."

"It wasn't."

"No. But by then I was in deep. We were going to my house when the cop who'd hit him drove up beside us. He jumped out and pulled his gun and Darrick didn't move or anything, but his mind did what it does, pushed back against his fear and anger. The cop's head swelled and shifted and next thing we knew, he dropped dead in the snow."

"So Darrick, too, has killed."

Lourana nodded. "But — "

"The Kavanaghs are one thing, and Darrick is another."

She was starting to regret her willingness to talk. *He's not on our side.* But what had she said that the Kavanaghs didn't already know anyway?

He leaned forward and held out his hands, palms up. Reluctantly, she rested her hands on his. She looked at that medallion hanging from its chain and thought, *amulet, I'd call that an amulet.*

"I know you are suspicious of me, and rightly so. What my intentions are. What my gifts are."

What am I doing? Lourana started to pull her hands away, but he held them.

"I'll let you see as I see."

Her vision was overcast with gray, like she was in a heavy fog, and then Rory stood before her. His body was a fragile cage around a smoky fire, a flickering assembly of flames that rose and fell and were sometimes obscured.

That vision was replaced by one of Darrick. He stood alone on a stone pinnacle, everything around him black, above, below, a world of absence.

Then she saw herself. She stood in the center of a ruined tower, the stone walls once strong but broken and patched. With one hand she was adding blocks, while with the other she removed them.

"What was that?" She yanked her hands free.

"How I see the world. My training guides me to understand through metaphor and symbols."

"I get Rory. And Darrick, he's an orphan and feels alone in the world." She paused. "Guess he is, now."

The druid regarded her for a long moment. "You have learned to protect yourself, and you fiercely protect family. That's your power but also your weakness, when you put up barriers to protect yourself that also shut out those you love."

Lourana was shaken by his insight, and ashamed a bit too, as she thought of the arguments she'd had with Darrick and Dreama and even her parents. She stood and went to the sink, ran a cup of water. It tasted of minerals, like water she remembered from a spring high on a mountain. It seemed alive. The window above the sink looked into the night forest as hers had done in Redbird. The nights she'd stood in the kitchen and looked out into nothing, wondering if her daughter would ever come home.

She remembered her last call with Dreama, when she admitted that she'd been meeting Rory "a time or two."

Lourana's whole body shook. "You can't be serious. You know what he is."

"He's Cormac."

"A lot more than that. Eamon, the grandfather. The whole vile brood. He only lets you see Cormac for his own purposes."

"I trust Cormac. And Rory."

She'd ended the call before her frustration could snap out at Dreama. Her daughter's last words had been faith in the Kavanaghs. And now she couldn't call, and her phone was somewhere silenced and unanswered.

The druid came up and stood beside her.

"Things need to come back to balance. However and wherever the Kavanaghs gained this power, it's inimical to the very life-force of the earth, animals and plants and people. Darrick's power also is ancient and unusual, and he may indeed carry a legacy from the rule-givers of old. The brehons were powerful in Celtic society, keepers of the peace and the interpreters of the law, even against the chieftains themselves. So we are akin in our intentions, though he doesn't understand the what or why."

"And what does a druid do?"

"Work between worlds, with fire and water, healing and inspiration."

Lourana tried to puzzle all this into a world that made sense. The picture wouldn't come together. "What now?"

"There is a saying, in the Jewish wisdom literature — there is a time to every purpose. We are waiting on that time. I will take you to a safe place, a holy place."

Lourana put that in her heart along with the rest of his vague pronouncements. He was the avenue to reaching Darrick, he'd said, and she'd go along but did not at all trust him. So she built walls? Block by block, she was rebuilding the emotional wall that had served before to shield her from the Kavanaghs — and might again with this Forest Sage.

Chapter 26

Darrick searched within the church, quickly, then went out and roved in circles around the building, stumbling through the graveyard by the light of his phone, rattling doors that all were locked, peering into windows that all were dark. No sign of her. He went back in and looked in every corner, pulled back curtains, ranged through the sacristy, investigated nooks. She was not there. Outside, he circled again, and wider. The sounds of the city went on in the background but he might as well have been in a wilderness. Finally, worn out and drenched with sweat, he got the car and went back to the hotel because he could think of nowhere else to go.

He sat on the bed and kept recasting the incident. What could he have done? How did he let Rory slip away? How did he let Lourana be taken?

He was knifed by his recent coldness toward her. The incident with the ring had hurt him so deeply that he'd retreated, and her efforts to draw him out went unheeded. How had she turned away from him? How had he lost her, emotionally and then physically?

He'd seen Cathbad take her arm, guide her away as he was confronting Rory. Cathbad, who had stood between him and Rory, and somehow had blunted both the Kavanagh powers and his own. He was at the center of this. What was his game?

The room closed around him, so still, and he was repelled at the thought of turning down the covers and climbing into bed without Lourana, as though that would be a betrayal. So he fell asleep in the chair, and woke in a dream of the story he'd read, in that heavy book left behind at Killeshandra, about the children of Lir, cursed by their stepmother to wander the island as wild swans for hundreds of years. Without Lourana, he felt as lost, buffeted by sea and storm. Without hope.

He kept checking his phone. He thought about calling Dreama, but he couldn't face telling her that he had somehow lost Lourana.

Finally, when it was 4 a.m., 9 a.m. in Redbird, Darrick did a search and got the number to KCL.

A woman's smooth voice. "Mr. Kavanagh is out of the office on business. May I take a message?"

None that Darrick could leave.

Chapter 27

He ran because concentration muted the committee in his head. He ran to avoid thinking about Darrick. He ran to shunt aside the latest updates from the lawyers about the multi-pronged investigations into KCL. You'll not face criminal penalties personally, they assured him, because you were not yet involved in the business, but officers and employees could. And the civil liabilities — well.

He'd covered the city end to end, waiting again for word from Cathbad and trying to outpace his life. The sweat filming his body, blown dry by the sea wind, forming again as he finished another mile — it made him feel like a whole being for a while.

Sometime between yesterday morning when he'd taken this same loop across the river islands and this evening, striped tents had sprouted like toadstools along the road. He ran in place for a minute, looking at the blinking fat bulbs outlining the sign, "Fun Fair," then decided against completing his route and instead jogged into the grounds.

The rides were turning in that desultory way when customers were few. He didn't suppose rain was all that much of a deterrent here, but it was raining steadily and the gaudy plastic was bright and shiny and slick. People were walking around, couples and families, kids ranging loose. The rain was turning the paths into mud. Distorted songs competed from booths and rides, and the smoke from grilled sausages and fried potatoes hung low and pungent. "Helter Skelter" was the sign on an openwork tower. "Big Dipper" and "Ice Jet" and a Ferris wheel and, oddly enough, an Indiana Jones ride with the sepiatoned faces of Harrison Ford and Sean Connery glowering above a phalanx of screaming children. It was as alien a place as any he'd seen in Ireland.

The carousel, surprisingly, was a fine old machine, the wooden horses carved with nostrils flaring and eyes wide as though pursued by tigers. On the panels of the central machinery, mirrors were mounted and lined with rows of bulbs, flashing out of synch with the wheezing music. As the carousel turned, horses rose and fell between him and his wavering shape in the mirrors. Just a shape. His face was lost inside the hood of his jacket.

He couldn't remember ever going to a circus or carnival, even when he was very young. Not with mother, nanny, classmates. Certainly not with his father.

A pair of teenagers walked past, carefully side by side, their steps matching, silent, not touching. Back home, they would have been entwined, hands pushed into each other's back pockets so they would be drawn together at the hip. And kissing as though they would devour the flesh as well as the breath. Rory thought he liked this reticence more.

Perhaps you're like the one in Dundalk, Eamon taunted.

He remembered the unusual psychic flavor of that victim, between male and female. He wondered if his father was right. Years spent in all-boy prep schools, with the usual outlets. Only the most superficial encounters with women during college, fearing his father's wrath if he became "entangled." Cormac's passion for Dreama had shown him something different, yet he'd never known that depth of need and desire for anyone. Male or female.

Cormac's presence, suffused with longing.

Patrick, his grandfather, blustered forward. *We must finish this. Then you will find a suitable wife and create an heir.*

What if it's a girl?

Kavanaghs sire only colts. Eamon's contempt lashed him. *And Kavanaghs don't run.*

Rory burned with the shame of having panicked in the church, fled from an attacking Darrick, but he could not have withstood the terrible power that had crushed him, if only for a moment.

You ran from Darrick, his father and grandfather chorused.

He would have killed us.

We are stronger, came the reply. *The druid will help.*

Rory become lost in his interior struggle. He shook himself and water flew from his jacket. The rain had increased and gotten colder, chilling him, and it was getting dark. He turned toward the hotel.

Eamon was a dark coal searing Rory's thoughts. *We will feed.*

He protested, Not so soon! All but Cormac were eager, pressing on him, pushing him forward. Even Padraig, whom he'd first encountered as a somnolent presence in the background, was day by day increasingly audible, rough-edged, brutal.

The girl he'd seen earlier at the Fun Fair was walking alone on the other sidewalk. Her head was bent, perhaps only from the rain, but maybe in sadness. The boy was nowhere to be seen. He coughed and she turned toward him.

"I'm an American," he said.

"Oh sure, I can tell that." Her voice was light, and yes, sad.

"I've gotten a bit turned around." He was impelled to cross the street to her.

Rain had beaded on her hair below her hat and it shone in the streetlights. Her face was wet, maybe from the rain, but he thought she had been crying.

"Might you show me the way to Eyre Square?"

She laughed. "You're going well enough already — keep on and you'll see it's at the city center." She was younger than he'd thought, maybe 15 or 16.

She's a child, he protested. Nevertheless, his feet moved and his hands, as he covered her mouth and guided her into an alley.

The others had control. They, he, held her closely as the light pulsed. He had to watch her face stiffen in terror as life was pulled from her. Slowly. The others wanted to punish him. Wanted him to experience every moment as her eyes dulled and her body collapsed in on itself and slid from his arms to the pavement.

Rory backed away, looked left and right, wishing someone had witnessed, that someone would take him, take his life, end this.

Time you become a proper Kavanagh, my fine lad. Padraig.

Rory began to run, again. As though he could outpace the evil within.

He remembered the first time.

He had been home for Christmas break, spending most of time in his room under pretext of books he was required to read. One afternoon, his grandfather Patrick summoned him to the library. He toured him around the family history, pointing out photographs and awards and certificates of various sorts. He showed him a florid certificate awarding the Order of the 35th Star, signed by A. James Manchin. "Ah, now there's a family of strivers. From the immigrant boat to the coal face to the halls of government. They'll allow a skiff of black dust upon their boots, to win the common man, but we honor the power that lies in the coal."

And that was how he had learned of the family crypt, cut into the rich Pittsburgh Seam that was the foundation of the mansion, and the family. His grandfather took him down to the basement, then down the narrow staircase. Unlocked a heavy door. Showed him the bones of his ancestors, laid out on biers of solid coal, and told their stories. Rory remembered studying the skeletons with the fascination of a 10-year-old boy.

"Why aren't they in the cemetery?" He was puzzled, having stood beside his father to lay wreaths at the monuments.

"Kavanaghs don't rest under dirt. We draw our life from this coal, and when that time is finished — well, there is more you will learn, in due time, but know that your forefathers remain part of your life."

They climbed from the secret sub-basement into the working areas under the house, where the cooks and laundresses and other servants labored. It was a steamy world smelling of bleach and boiling potatoes and roasting meat. His grandfather caught the eye of a rotund man peeling apples at a sink. "If you'd serve us, please, in the breakfast room." The cook set down his knife and followed, but Rory saw him pick up no plates or napkins.

In the room, tree-shadowed in the afternoon, his grandfather touched the man on the shoulder, and with the other hand grasped Rory's wrist.

At first he felt only his grandfather's dry fingers, but then something strange happened. He watched a thin ribbon of light pass from the cook into his grandfather, and that energy flowed onward through his hand and into Rory's body.

"I'm scared," he whispered as his heart jumped.

"Can you feel it? The life force?"

He nodded. "I want it to stop." His pulse pounded in his grandfather's grip and he felt as though he was expanding, growing but not in the way the nanny tracked with a pencil on the measuring wall.

"Only a taste." His grandfather dismissed the cook with a nod and he went back to his kitchen without a word.

They sat at the table where they took eggs and toast in the mornings. Rory understood that what had just happened was food, a different sort of food, and he vibrated with energy like when he'd eaten too much chocolate.

"It does not hurt them," his grandfather explained. "We take just enough to boost our essential natures, and our connection to these people actually lengthens their lifespans."

Rory tried to find a way to make what seemed very wrong into something right. "It's like sharing," he said at last.

"Yes, yes," his grandfather said, and laughed. "You did well, my fine lad."

Now he recognized the echo of Padraig in that voice.

Chapter 28

It was an indelible image: Lourana pulling the ring from her finger like it had scorched her, then turning it around to indicated she wasn't all that committed to him. Not yet, she'd said. *Probably not ever.* Darrick saw the green stone catch the light in what for him was a romantic moment. Saw her twist the ring back off, glance at him as though he was an overeager teenager, then thrust it back on reversed.

"That don't mean all the way," she'd said.

Not yet. Over and over.

He thought driving would at least give him something else to concentrate on, so he headed north with no particular itinerary, taking the roads as they branched right so that perhaps he'd make a circle. There was always the map, but he couldn't even look at that, for remembering. It was a blustery, cold day with a leaden sky spitting rain across the gray bulk of eroded mountains and wind-whipped loughs.

Perfect.

Even the charmingly named towns seemed unwelcoming, Ardcong and Castlerea and Ballinameen. Cars were parked along the streets but the sidewalks mostly empty and gutters bubbling with runoff. Even the pubs with warm yellow light pouring through the windows didn't beckon.

He was almost into Northern Ireland when he remembered about the insurance, so he turned back at the edge of Blacklion and along the returning route saw a sign for "Cavan Burren Park" and on a whim turned in. He'd learned about burrens, bleak windswept limestone plateaus where plants grew in the cracks of the stone. *Perfect.* He pulled his windbreaker hood up and stepped out into the driving wet.

A large map indicated the trails were not very long, so he headed up the Giant's Leap path, only to find this wasn't the raw, exposed burren he was expecting. It was green with tussocky grass and shamrocks and bushes and pine trees, but also huge boulders lying about, and mysterious gatherings of stone. A raised path crossed a bog. *If I stepped off here, maybe they'd find my body in 2,000 years, nicely tanned.* This was where legendary brothers had competed for the love of a woman, and one lost. The giant fell into the Giant's Leap valley and was buried under the wedge tomb. It was a tomb fit for a giant, an enormous slab of stone canted up on another, the interior closed with rubble.

No bones rested in the wedge tomb, giant or warrior or chieftain.

He stepped inside on the flat blocks laid down for that purpose, he guessed. It was a cold space, with enough light through the entrance that ferns grew along the base of the walls. It probably was long used as a shelter by whoever had to cross this terrain. Or maybe not. Perhaps people came to leave offerings, flowers. Or maybe shunned these sites as places inhabited by spirits and demons. If a giant's bones had been there, they were long gone.

Darrick had never thought of his own skeleton really, in his body, until he woke up among the dead. Down in that cave, no, mine crack, he'd picked up bones, a skull, and in the inspiration that drives survival, smashed the ends of femurs into climbing sticks to anchor in the sides of the hole and slowly pull himself to safety. But the weight and feel of his bones, the body's framework, was something he'd simply accepted. The spine held up the body, but until he saw the naked bones of the Kavanaghs laid out in the crypt, he hadn't considered how elegant a spine was, the vertebrae. Bare sculptural things. The eyes and lips, the brains, the soft of the belly, all the vulnerable parts, all gone.

He felt that the soft parts of his life had been stripped away, leaving only the stony framework.

He went back out and sat with his back to a vertical wall of the tomb on the lee side from the wind. No other hikers on this unpleasant day. No sound but the wind, tuning its voice in the tomb. He looked around, waited to feel some connection to this land that his DNA claimed was home. Nothing. He didn't belong here. He didn't belong anywhere.

The problem was thinking that his essentially solitary life could be changed. First he'd fallen for Nicole and thought she would make his world complete. When she left, it wasn't so difficult to reacquaint himself with his old habits. Then that wrong-exit decision that sent him into places he'd never expected, and into the arms of Lourana. He saw her as she'd revealed herself to him that night, not just physically but emotionally, daring to let her positive emotions clang against his deadly psychic shield, trusting that he would not respond or could control his response.

He couldn't get his mind around the change in Lourana. The things they'd experienced together he thought had bonded them beyond any parting, yet had she begun pulling away from him even before they came to Ireland. He traced those small moments, the irritations, the assessing glances.

So here he was, turning to stone himself it seemed, growing cold and hard as he sat against the tomb wall and felt himself scoured. Bereft. Alone.

He'd had enough therapy to recognize how he was wallowing in self-pity, but didn't care. He'd learned to cope without parents, without family, and for a long time, without love. That had made him vulnerable. Nicole had said she loved him. So had Lourana. But he'd lost her even before Cathbad or Rory or both took her away at the church.

The thought of her with Rory. With Eamon.

Rainwater trickled down the stones, nourishing little plants that grew in the cracks, sending down roots, raising up tiny flowers.

They managed. It made him think of Lourana, surviving in the unwelcoming landscape of Carbon County.

Darrick pushed himself to his feet and started the rest of the loop trail back to the visitor's center and his car.

He saw a stone with cups ground into the surface and circled by incised rings. As old as the tombs, he guessed. It made him think of Cathbad, and he wondered what a latter-day druid had to do with such ancient landscapes. Did those beliefs extend back to the Stone Age, to people who labored to make these symbols? Had druids levitated the stones of the dolmens and tombs, or just brute human labor? Those ancient people must have lived on the edge of famine always, looked for their gods in the earth and sky, but finding no help from them. Even if they were savages wearing animal skins, they were human, and must have felt the kind of misery he knew now. Even giants, killing themselves to win a woman.

Darrick got to the visitor's center, bypassing the exhibits on his way to the restrooms. He was a wet mess but it didn't matter.

In the car, he checked the time and realized he'd driven well more than two hours, back into Cavan County where Killeshandra was. He turned toward Galway. A place he no longer wanted to be.

Should he abandon Lourana before she finished letting him go? She was kind, under that tough surface, and would probably find it difficult to take the final step.

It would be doing her a favor, to cut the cord, move on without her. She could go back to West Virginia and her daughter and make some kind of a normal life. Of course, he'd have to find her first.

Then he would find the Kavanaghs, or let them find him, more likely, and end it one way or the other.

Chapter 29

"Are you a Christian?"

Lourana was taken aback. She remembered being accosted by street preachers, shouting and waving floppy Bibles. Marrying and burying was the only time her family had gone to church, nominally Christian in a mountain culture where people were identified by kin first and then by church and then by their place on the land.

"No. Not so much."

"I didn't think so. There's an aura to them."

They passed another car and Cathbad raised his hand in acknowledgement, as did the other driver.

"Do you know him?"

"No, it's just common courtesy."

"We do the same thing in West Virginia."

"I believe our peoples are a lot alike. A love for home, and persistence in the face of terrible odds. Of course, a lot of Irish are to be found in your state."

Like Kavanaghs, she thought.

They'd left the cottage, which Cathbad said belonged to one of his students, tidy as they'd found it, with two cups washed and set on the sink board. Breakfast was a frosted roll from a little store. "We have a fair drive ahead of us," he told her. She asked herself why she hadn't tried to sneak out in the night. Fear? Not really. Enchantment? Unlikely. Of a piece with auras. But lacking a phone, car, or anything, she hadn't come up with a better plan than staying with Cathbad, keeping an eye on him until he brought her back to Darrick. For now.

Their route headed east, across the island from Galway toward Dublin but then turning south at Athlone. It had been less than three hours when they pulled off at a patch of forest beside a lake. A few cars were parked in the lot where a trail entered the woods.

"I was expecting a longer drive," she said as she got out and stretched.

"We're a wee place, compared to your United States. I've heard it said that Ireland is the size of your own West Virginia." His voice was muffled as he reached under the hatchback of the little car and brought out an Adidas duffel bag. He reached in again and hauled out a walking stick, or really, you'd have to call it a staff. Oak leaves were carved into it below a smooth knob at the top. Lourana remembered what he'd said, that the word for oak had become druid. And Darrick.

They followed a mulched path from the parking lot. It plunged into spring woodlands where birds sang and trees were bright with that new green of leaves not yet worn out by the year. A wooden sign noted the distance for the trail.

"Isn't this a public park?"

"Aren't we the public?" He turned and smiled at her. "But yes, it is. Grove is the name for a congregation — like church, it's about people, not place. We don't generally own the forests where we meet, the way you would a building."

He abruptly stepped off the groomed path, following some sign she couldn't recognize. After a little bit, she could see a narrow path appearing like an animal trail. Small white flowers showed among the grass — and shamrocks! Those were shamrocks!

"Private ownership of the land was an innovation brought by the conquerors," said Cathbad, marching ahead and lecturing as usual. "Traditionally, the tribes of Eire held their territory in common under a chief." She tore herself away from the flowers and ran after him, almost colliding with him when he stopped to examine white mushrooms sprouting from the bole of a downed tree.

They entered a clearing. To one side, a small fire burned in a portable fire pot. Two men and a woman waited there, each holding a green branch. She recognized the leaves of ash and oak.

Cathbad unzipped the duffel bag and took out a long robe that he pulled over his regular clothes. He struggled to extract the amulet and settle it outside his robe.

"Costumes?" she whispered.

"As a matter of fact, yes. It's as sacred a ceremony as any in the pope's domain, so should we not observe it with solemnity?" His robe swept the ground as he moved to join the others, and she saw it was dirty all around the bottom. He either used it a lot or didn't much care about laundry.

A second woman appeared from the lefthand side. Like the others, she was dressed in ordinary clothes, and held a branch, something thorny. The participants glanced at the sky, cloudless blue for once, and spaced themselves equally around a circle, between the fire at one pole and Cathbad at the other.

"Good morning my friends. We gather here for a ceremony of healing for the land and the people, grievously wounded." He raised his staff and they raised their branches. "Welcome to our grove this guest Lourana. She has been a guardian of rivers."

"Welcome," they said in unison, and then, "fáilthe."

She bowed her head, not sure what was appropriate.

"We honor this season of springing, when the world is restored." Cathbad's voice had taken on a different tone.

A response came, in another language.

"We celebrate Brighid, who rules over both fire and water."

The response, again, in what she expected must be Irish.

"We honor Brighid, who brings poetry to our hearts and healing to our souls."

Another response.

"Together, we bow before the life-force that flows through every being."

From there, Lourana was lost. Cathbad also began to speak in that other tongue. She wondered if he had begun in English for her benefit. The group circled, made gestures with their branches, and she heard "Brighid" repeated several times. Something was cast on the fire that sizzled and smelled piney, like fatwood as you started a fire, then something else and it gave off a spicy scent.

It had seemed comical at first, especially Cathbad in his grimy robe and a staff like a wizard in a low-budget fantasy movie, but as the ceremony progressed, Lourana felt moved by it. The bright faces of the people, the rise and fall of a chant that became soothing as waves breaking on a beach, and she realized that she could no longer hear the shrieks of children elsewhere in the park, nor the sound of cars and trucks.

Cathbad moved to the center and spread his arms wide. He raised the staff and the others raised their branches. They sang together and the fire leaped up, one, twice, three times. Their branches seemed to glow from within. Or maybe she was imagining things.

Then it was over. One of the men put out the fire pot and carried it away. Cathbad took off his robe, rolled it and stashed it in the duffel. The people of the grove disappeared into the woods along other trails, and the sounds of children and traffic and barking dogs resumed. Or maybe she was imagining things.

As they made their way out, she saw the quick movements of small birds, heard their piping calls and thought "chickadee," but these were brighter, with yellow on their tiny bodies, and that one had a blue head! And a bird with the red breast of a robin, but nothing like that bird in its shape. Things were the same here, or sort of, but different.

"Everything is so gorgeous. Birds and flowers and trees. Just like this documentary I watched," she said. "But you were talking about the land being wounded. Not like what I've seen back home."

"These places are fragments," he said as he backed the car out of the space. "Grantstown Wood and Coolacurragh Wood, just small bits of what Ireland should look like. This is a native forest of ash and birch and alder and hawthorn, and brambles and meadowsweet and stinging nettles — we used those, and oak, for the healing ceremony today. But most of Ireland is no longer forested, or if it is, then with foreign conifers. Tree farms that don't support the ecosystem."

"But it's all so — green."

"Those forty shades of green people are always going on about. It is that, but with Sitka spruce in plantations. And cropland, and grazings. Places turned to moor that were once forest."

Lourana couldn't figure how things were so bad when it seemed beautiful. What had happened to all the trees? But she didn't want to spark another lecture so she watched the scenery, damaged or not, flow past. The druid remained silent until they stopped for "petrol" and a snack.

"I'm sorry to disabuse you of your view of my beloved island," he said after filling the tank. "It's not hopeless. At one time less than two percent of Ireland wore its own trees, and that's now been tripled. We plant, and tend, and give ourselves to the restoration."

"So you're kind of an Earth religion."

"We're the original Earth religion. Planting trees and cleaning up rivers is a worthy thing, and we take part, but our mission also goes deeper."

"That balance thing."

"Yes. The world's losing its beat, its tempo. The fruit trees are scorched by late frost after heat. The summers are hotter and the fields bake under sun. Even in the ocean, the fish migrate at the wrong time and the seabirds starve."

Lourana wolfed down a sack of chips and a sort of hot dog. She watched him work his way through a similar sack of chips — crisps — but no meat. You probably had to be a vegetarian to be a druid. She wanted to ask him about the fire, about the glowing branches, but wondered if she'd give offense. Maybe it was like the Masons, you joined with a terrible oath not to reveal the innermost secrets.

"You're curious."

"Of course."

"We're not sworn to secrecy over a naked blade," he said, his eyes doing that thing again, and she blushed to think that he'd read her thoughts.

They sorted their cups and wrappers into the bins and got back into the car.

"The ceremony you just saw is admittedly a recent invention. The original Orders were driven to extinction, rather like the wolf and the wildcat, at least in England and Wales. Much druidical lore persisted under the guise of folk tales and Christianized festivals. Eventually, the bits and bobs were expanded into a modern version of druidry. For some people, this is costumed theater, something interesting to do at Midsummer and Samhain. But there has always been a thread, however fragile, reaching back to the original forms and the actual powers of the ancients. I am one of those kinds of druids, though many would take me for no more than a showman."

Again, Lourana wondered how much he could know of her thoughts. *Too much.*

"I studied and worked for many years, decades, rising through the levels of skill to grasp the responsibilities of the name. Within the Order, we have poets, or bards, who are vessels for inspiration. Next are the ovates, who are dedicated to healing. A druid is charged with care of the sacred fire, within the body, within the grove, within creation."

"So I did see the fire, the branches . . ."

He nodded. "You are perceptive, my dear. Yes, you saw a part."

"How did you choose to get tangled up with the Kavanaghs?"

"Purely by chance. Rory and his ancestors, though I hadn't met them at that point, were visiting an ancient site that they believe is linked to their family. I was there with students of the craft. When I first met the young man, I thought, here's another wealthy American come to drop some cash on the Old Sod, and I was ready to play his fantasies along to get funding for our trees. But when I shook his hand, I was dismayed by a sense of utter wrongness. There is something perverted in the Kavanaghs that allows them to grasp life itself, extract life, and to persist across generations."

"They devour people."

"I am starting to understand. The surfacing of the ancestors was — horrific. And puzzling. How did they come by this talent? So I attached myself to Rory, to them, with promises of aid."

"You're playing both sides against the middle."

"Isn't the middle the balance point of any scale? I'm always on the side of balance and restoration. The Kavanaghs are an abomination."

"I'm glad you can see that."

"There's much to learn, if you pay attention." He clicked on his blinker and turned. "Don't you feel that the world is out of balance? That each of us has helped to shift it, just a hair, and now we must do our part to bring it back?"

"That's global warming, not the Kavanaghs." She thought about the Norfolk Southern trains, loaded with KCL coal, following the path of the river out of West Virginia to be burned and add to the problem.

"Everything's connected. The Kavanaghs certainly can't be blamed for all that's amiss in the world, but they are a part of it. Maybe what damage we've done to our Earth has led to the creation of monsters, who'll extract a terrible toll on humans who've been so greedy."

"And Darrick?"

"He's tapped into something from ancient times as well. His name says 'son of the judge' but at first glance seems to me more akin to the powers of the ancient ollave, the high poets whose moral pronouncements, issued in satire, could shrivel a king. The source of his gift seems to be clean, but he doesn't know how to employ it, or when."

That's not a ringing endorsement.

Lourana wanted to think this man was a genuine mystic, commanding the powers of nature, but she remembered how his face looked when he got between Rory and Darrick. It had looked a lot like panic.

"If you have a handle on this secret fire, then why can't you get rid of the Kavanaghs?"

"If it were only a matter of the ghosts who rattle around his body, then I would try, but there's a living person involved."

"Rory? He's one of them."

"He's a human being, my dear, whose life has value, and who may be salvaged."

They had reached the main highway, but they didn't turn back to Galway.

"Where are we going?"

"To Brighid's house."

Chapter 30

The woman just shook her head as Darrick approached.

The spartan room in Killeshandra was the last they'd shared in happiness, and it seemed like the place where Lourana might look for him, if she could. He'd left the hotel in Galway with word about his location, and contacted the manse in Dublin, but came back here to wait. For what, he didn't know.

Still, Darrick couldn't bring himself to walk on the forest path or eat at their favorite pubs, so he foraged the aisles of the Today's Extra market for whatever could be reconstituted with boiling water from the kettle. He still didn't know if this Cathbad person had Lourana, or worse yet, Rory, but his phone never lit up with her face or played the first bars of "Country Roads."

He wasn't trying to hide any longer. The rental car sat out front. Let the Kavanaghs come. He would give himself gladly, every particle, if it pried her loose from their clutches. Was she still wearing the ring, he wondered, and had her mind changed? She'd allowed herself to be led off, so passively. Or maybe she went willingly, seeing a way to cut herself loose from him without having to say so to his face.

Darrick sat by the pond, watching the ducks dabble and cows move slowly up and down the green slope, or wandered the town. He stopped by the remains of a church and walled graveyard in the lower end. It was off balance, it seemed, and he realized that was not built in the usual shape of a cross but was T-shaped, truncated. At night he read an appalling book about the Hunger, the workhouses, the coffin ships. Somewhere among the desperate people of that diaspora lay his ancestry, or so it seemed. The drawings woke him in the bleak dawn, hollow-eyed figures shuffling in their rags through his dreams.

As the day wore on, and his restlessness wouldn't be quelled, he went out driving again. On the Portaliffe Road, he passed St. Brigid's Church. Half a mile down the road, he U-turned and went back.

They'd visited a succession of these stone churches with their gothic windows, but this time, he didn't glance around like a tourist and leave. The interior was painted yellow, which gave him a shudder as he recalled the night at St. Nicholas, but he went to the stoup, touched his fingers to the holy water and made the signum salutis.

The church had images of the Holy Mother and St. Brigid. He dropped a coin in the box and lit a candle before each one. *Women and protectors of women, protect Lourana.*

Darrick slid into a back pew. As the day faded, people began coming in for Mass. He couldn't remember the last time he'd attended. His angry heart, to say nothing of his blackened soul, was not in a proper spiritual condition to receive any sort of grace, but he stayed.

Chapter 31

Rory had once been asked, while he sat on the colorful rug in the school library, what superpower he would wish for could he choose one. Immediately he had answered, "Be invisible!"

"That's a very good choice! Why would you want that superpower?"

He couldn't answer, that a cloak of invisibility would allow him to avoid his father's eye. Even then he knew that he didn't measure up, that his father's glance found him wanting. Year by year, his excellent grades in school were proof only that he might become a useless dilettante like his uncle. His achievements in cross-country were considered paltry compared with proper sports such as football or hockey or rugby. Contact sports, where a man was bloodied. Now Eamon might be dead, in the eyes of the world, but he had if anything a greater capacity to torment Rory for his failings.

You have a reverse Frankenstein problem. Cormac. He flashed a memory of the classic movie, the eager doctor and his henchman digging up a fresh body for the laboratory.

How so? asked Rory.

*The doctor created life, but was disappointed in his handiwork.
Yet the monster lived, and pursued the father who would not give him
a name.*

My father created me, but I refused my father's name for me.

And you would flee from him.

If I could.

Rory was intrigued by the insights his uncle provided, most of
the time, though it was strange to feel Cormac becoming so deeply
twined into his "self" awareness. He feared that embracing his uncle's
spirit was hastening the inevitable moment when Eamon ferreted out
his secret. For now, he hid only occasionally, and not for too long, lest
Eamon become suspicious and come digging for his reluctant heir.

Or perhaps you find yourself more akin to Hamlet.

Rory heard a powerful British voice, Olivier's he guessed, intoning, "Do you not come your tardy son to chide, / That, laps'd in time
and passion, lets go by / Th' important acting of your dread command?"

That dread command appeared with regularity, *Avenge me!
Avenge me!*, even as Eamon pressed his search for regal roots. But
Rory's lack of success in killing Darrick, so far, was not Eamon's only
grievance with his heir. Rory had failed to come quickly enough to
his bedside for the transfer to be completely accomplished. Eamon was
well aware of the gaps in his memory, and how he lapsed into incoherence as words refused to come.

You let them take me.

That bitter complaint also rose regularly. Once the police had
been notified and the contents of the crypt discovered, there had been
no way for the butler, or Rory, or any earthly power to keep Eamon at
Knockaulin House so that a proper ending could be accomplished and
his bones entombed beside those of his fathers.

You let them take my body.

The hospital oversaw his dying, and then a funeral home was
required. While they'd been able to prevent the further violation of
embalming, forensic tests were mandated and tissue removed, followed
by a speedy burial beside the impressive Kavanagh monument. A monument looted from Ireland to preside over empty coffins.

In the dirt. Eamon raged at the indignity, and his ancestors
joined him. *Buried in the dirt.*

Yet here you are, Rory replied, all the stronger for having devoured your father and brother.

I was prepared. Patrick. *It was time.*

And wasn't he draining you of life before it was time, Grandfather? And Cormac? It certainly wasn't his time.

Cormac was neutered. Eamon. *Until he brought home the woman.*

And you feared he might escape?

Could not allow another dynasty.

You could have let us go away. Cormac.

Why not, Eamon? Why did Cormac have to die?

You will call me Father.

His father's displeasure cracked like a whip against his back.

You do not have to love me. Respect.

What more can you do to me? You cannot kill me.

I can own you entirely.

Rory knew that was true. That Eamon could use his body like a puppet, and not just when he demanded to feed — could gain another life by living through him without regard for his wishes. So could Padraig, Domnall. Even Cormac.

He saw one small spark of hope, if you could call it that. The Kavanagh legacy had a starting point. It reached only back to Padraig, not to an endless line of fathers extending back into legend. And if he could manage it, there would be a stopping place as well. The chain of father to son must be broken at some point, if not with him then another. Privately, he swore never to marry, never to make another Kavanagh on the earth.

That might have been laughter he heard, within.

If we were believers, we might fear the eventual destination of our spirits, said Cormac. *As the king's ghost said, "My hour is almost come / When I to sulph'rous and tormenting flames / Must render up myself."*

Chapter 32

She'd been promised a house, but what she got was another church.

They arrived early, while mists still lay on the lands around Kildare Town, so green and lush that again she thought Cathbad was exaggerating. Expensive horses grazed behind board fences. It reminded her of Kentucky when she and Steve took a vacation trip there once. The sun came up a fiery pink through bands of clouds that streamed across the sky, shadowing the landscape then blowing apart.

Cathbad had been uncharacteristically silent as they drove. They came to a big church that was hemmed in by houses, as though the town had huddled close for protection. The church, St. Brigid's, was pretty similar to others, but there was an interesting round tower standing alone. Tall and skinny, like a good storm might blow it over. The graveyard sprouted those Celtic crosses with haloes.

As they parked, he turned to her. The sun through the windshield struck his amulet, and in that slanting light she saw for the first time that it was covered with circles engraved with fine lines, with a flame image at the center.

"I'm going to ask you to do something difficult." The twinkle was gone from his deep-set eyes. "You can refuse."

"And if I do?"

"Then I cannot think of any way to disentangle your fate from that of the Kavanaghs, short of death."

She waited, keyed up by his serious mood.

"I have brought you here, where Brighid holds sway and female energy is strong. I will let you know more about that. But the why of it — I want you to meet with Rory."

"Oh, no thank you, *SIR!* Not again," Lourana's hand drifted toward the door handle. A sudden memory flashed of holding Dreama's chubby hand and explaining "stranger danger."

"Hear me out." His voice was strong and a little loud. *Trying that glamour on me again?* "I promised you that I would try to find a way to heal this — situation. And I promised Rory, who is trapped even more than you and Darrick."

"Can I tell you how much I don't care?"

He waited her out.

"Well, I don't much like being blindsided."

"Would you have come if I'd told you up front?"

She didn't answer, because he must know she realized that was true. She could feel the flush of anger still warming her cheeks and thought again about that image he shared, of herself standing within a stone wall and building it up even as she tore it down brick by brick. Her emotional defenses were weak, and here he was wanting her to stand face to face with the Kavanaghs. Alone, without Darrick.

"I am asking you to hear him out. He wants to have a truce. You will have my protection, and that of my grove, and Brighid herself."

"Magic tricks."

"Not mere magic. And not tricks. Brighid is as real as the very earth."

He got out and came around, took his staff from the back seat and opened her door. Now Lourana was reluctant to leave the small security of the vehicle.

"It pains me that you, who have experienced terrible forces not explained by either science or faith, should think that I would resort to illusions. You have seen a little bit of that power — few people can, by the by."

If she was supposed to feel ashamed, it wasn't working. Still, she remained stubbornly in her seat.

"I don't see how you can protect me."

"Although I bear the name of the greatest of all druids, I am well aware that I am not him. I use what slender powers have been granted to me to the utmost, and with Brighid's aid I will protect you."

He held out his hand and she took it (a bit glad for the help as the car was so low) and they went into the church.

"Come with me. See the church, and we'll talk of Brighid. Then you can decide. As I said, no compulsion."

As they entered the dim sanctuary she was blinded for a moment, after the bright sun. Then her eyes adjusted to the gray interior, the shafts of colored light from narrow windows.

"You already know about Brighid as a saint, if you were listening at the gallery. The Church is excellent at incorporating deities too great for it to destroy, as the Roman Empire did before it. There was no separating Brighid from the Irish, or the Irish from her, so they merged her cultus with that of a medieval saint. She was and she remains."

Cathbad was back to lecturing. He showed her Crusader tombs and a sculpture of a bony Christ with ropes around his wrists and a crown of thorns, but he always came around to Brighid. Here was an image of her. There, the woven cross, her sign which he said also represented the sun and the quarters of the year.

Lourana was half listening. She thought about Rory, that day at the office, how he seemed an ordinary man until his father pushed through that facade like high school football players bursting through a paper banner. She could imagine sitting down and talking with Rory. Not Eamon. Not ever.

She turned around and caught her breath at the dazzle of golden light pouring across the altar, thick as honey. The gray arches above her faded away to blue.

"So, you see," Cathbad said. "The flame of Kildare may have been extinguished by the church hierarchy, but the truth of it never died. The fire was taken away by the faithful and maintained in a secret location, and it burns still. All creation is suffused with that brightness."

"It's only the stained glass," she said, irritated.

"Do you think so?"

Lourana, as she stared at the glory, wasn't so sure.

"Come. Let's go to where the fire began."

She was expecting another building, but they went out to a hole in the ground, a square space like a double grave with stone walls and a plaque that said it had been reconstructed in 1988.

"Some say this is the location, but it's not correct," he said, glancing into the hole as they continued to walk around the hill. "The sacred fire on the hill of Kildare was tended by 19 women, with Brighid herself tending it on the 20th. Priestesses first, then nuns, from time immemorial until the 16th century."

He leaned against his staff like an ordinary walking stick. "Our lore says the fire temple was outside the compound. This spot is our best estimation."

She saw people coming, recognized two of them from the earlier ritual. Now there were more, six, seven, eight. They formed a circle around Cathbad and Lourana.

"We call upon Brighid in her role as peacemaker, who reconciled rival clans, and who brings peace between faiths." The grove replied, "Bring unity of spirit."

"Brighid holds those who are in danger in the palms of her hands. Brighid calms the great seas from their rage." And the response came, "Bring peace."

The chant continued, moving now into Gaelic. Lourana felt something, she wasn't sure what. Awe? Reassurance? A presence filled this place that was different from the Kavanaghs and Darrick. It was like the touch of her mother's hand on her fevered brow.

The people clasped hands, and a soft shimmer seemed to weave among them, the pale yellow-green of young leaves.

And there was Rory, approaching from the church, his red hair like a different and devouring flame. Had he been there all along? Watching them? She shuddered with a cold chill and moved a little apart from Cathbad.

Rory stopped almost at shouting distance.

"Remember that you are on doubly holy ground, to parlay only," Cathbad warned.

"What do you Kavanaghs have to say to me?" Lourana couldn't keep the rage out of her voice, and didn't try.

"I want an end," Rory said, his voice strained.

"You're the ones chasing us all over the map. We want to be left alone. Me. Darrick. Dreama."

"Will you mediate? Between Darrick and — us." His voice was pleading, and she could see the swift transitions of an interior struggle on his face, storm clouds racing and gathering menace.

"I am with Rory." *That was Cormac. How many people were inside there?*

Rory shuddered and stepped forward, then back. Again. His fists were clenched at his sides.

"Murderer." Eamon's harsh voice burst from Rory's mouth. His lean body seemed to hunch forward, as though suddenly burdened with muscle and bone, an illusion perhaps but the sense of the father's power over his son was not.

Rory began to advance on the circle, his tread oddly weighty. His eyes were wide, unfocused, and his feet snagged in the turf as though he couldn't sense where he walked. She expected him, them, to push through the tissue protection of the circle and take her life. And eventually Darrick's.

Cathbad raised his staff.

"Let the living speak and the dead keep silence," he roared. The circle of wan light flared to a rich greenish glow. She caught her breath at the sense of a great and beneficent power around her.

Rory halted and seemed to regain his own stance. For a little space, quiet. She could hear the hum of traffic in the town below, the chatter of birds, and somewhere a woman raised her voice above the shouts of children. Then Eamon seemed to regain ascendancy and Rory came on again. His eyes locked with hers and she could almost hear him saying, *I am trying to stop this.*

When he was close to the circle, the light did not break, but moved out and encompassed his body, enfolding him in its web. He seemed to relax in it, as though supported.

"Peace," he pleaded, and Cormac's elegant tones were twinned with Rory's voice. "Let us have peace."

Lourana wavered. She was terrified of Eamon but felt a pang of sympathy for the man who stood before her. The druid had proved, improbably, that he could contain the Kavanaghs. She did not think any longer that he was a fraud, but where did his sympathies lie in the end? Was the balance that precise?

On one hand, she could see a quick and final conclusion to the story. On the other, a chance to have a life free of fear, something other than this refugee wandering, which led to perhaps the same end after all. Could Cathbad end this spiral toward inevitable destruction?

"I will," she began, then, more sure of herself, "I will mediate, if Cathbad can protect us."

"With Brighid's help, I surely will," Cathbad said.

Rory nodded, and the green glow parted outward and gently released him. He stepped back, appearing to be younger, refreshed, as he turned away and loped toward the church. When they saw a car pull out and drive off, Cathbad set the foot of his staff against the ground and sagged against its support. The light went out quick as a candle snuffed; the members of the grove acknowledged their leader and then scattered.

Lourana felt the doubt creep back. *Maybe I'm putting too much faith in this wizard stuff.*

Chapter 33

Darrick thought he might be going crazy.

Maybe because he wasn't taking his medication as religiously as he'd always done, which led to the anticipated balance issues and staggering, but never before to hallucinations.

Maybe it was a legacy from getting his head bashed in back in West Virginia, an attack that had upended his life and brought him together with Lourana, and the Kavanaghs.

Maybe it was the lack of sleep. He couldn't stay down more than a couple of hours at a time, getting up in the black dark of 2 and 3:30 a.m., making tea, afraid to walk the creaking floors and disturb the unsmiling woman who'd let him take back the room, alone now, without a question. He couldn't focus on reading, not one of the books he'd chosen with such delight. He couldn't even focus on the squabbling ducks.

All he knew was that, as he slouched in the lumpy chair, he heard Lourana's voice as clearly as though she stood beside him: "I'm on my way, Darrick."

"On your way where?" No answer. "Here?"

Darrick looked at the black face of his phone, touched it awake. Nothing. He went outside and walked around the house, looked down the lane. Nothing.

So he went back to the uncomfortable chair, as good a place as any, and waited to see if any more messages materialized.

An hour later, he heard wheels crunching up the road. He ran to the door, out to the drive, and saw Lourana riding in a little car with a man driving — that Cathbad. She smiled and waved out the open window as though just returning from a trip to the market. As if nothing were wrong.

He just stood there, trembling, not sure what to expect since she'd disappeared with this guy and not a word since.

As soon as the car stopped, she was out the door and running, grabbed him and hugged him so hard she might have broken a rib. "I've been so worried about you!"

"Me?" He was taken aback by her enthusiastic greeting, after Galway.

"Yes! I didn't know what happened with you, at least right away."

"I've been worried about YOU. You left with him." He tried to keep the accusation out of his voice. "And your phone was off."

"I know. But so much has happened!"

"I think she'll assure you I was a perfect gentleman. I needed her full attention as we are engaged in a great work." From a pocket of his vest, Cathbad produced her phone and restored it with a flourish.

"Why? Why did you take her? Where did you go?" As Darrick could feel himself getting worked up, he was prepared for something similar from Cathbad, but he sensed nothing but emotional quiet, a mind placid as a lake. "You're working for the Kavanaghs."

"Darrick." Lourana touched his arm. "It's okay."

"It's far from okay."

"Listen to me. You know how I didn't understand what you did, even when I saw it happen. And the Kavanaghs, that was just a legend until . . ." Her voice trailed off.

The images that came to her mind must have been the same as his, the black room, Dreama huddled beside a skeleton, Marco's sacrifice.

"Well, I didn't believe that Cathbad was what he says he is, until I saw for myself. Darrick, he stopped Eamon. Stopped him in his tracks. Made him shut up and let Rory talk."

"He fooled you."

"No tricks. I've seen things, Darrick." She was passionate, her brows drawing down as she emphasized her point. "He says he's a druid, and I don't know much about that, but he controlled Eamon."

"Druid? Are you kidding me?"

Cathbad made a little half-smile and glanced at Lourana. "She will tell you more, but in essence, I work with the natural powers of the world."

Darrick felt Lourana's bubbling excitement, as though she believed this ridiculous man. He also felt her love. She stayed close to him, touching him as though she wasn't sure he was real. He was reassured to have her there, her arm pressed against his. It seemed her doubts had evaporated during the time they were separated. His, however, had not yet been dispelled.

Darrick caught the flick of a curtain, the landlady checking things out. There didn't seem to be anything left to do but go inside for a scanty tea.

This Cathbad, this so-called druid, as it turned out was more than happy with decaffeinated tea, as he took no stimulants. Lourana smiled to find sachets of Nescafe coffee in the bowl, ones he'd bought in hopes of her return.

They sat around the little table on mismatched chairs, so they were all at different heights. The armchair that Darrick used dropped him lower than Cathbad perched on a kitchen stool, who sipped his tea pensively, then set the cup aside.

"I need not tell you how dangerous the Kavanaghs are. Lourana has told me about their attacks, and how you respond to a threat."

"I have learned to control that."

"Perhaps. It's a talent as strange as theirs, and no less deadly."

Darrick couldn't prove anything one way or the other. At least not at the moment.

"They've accessed some kind of dark power beyond my ken. Still, I can draw upon resources enough to hold it at bay. From my experience, I'd say these Kavanaghs are like any family. They can't get along."

"We have two allies, Rory and his uncle," added Lourana. "They are doing their best to restrain Eamon and the rest."

"They are bound together in this hereditary vampirism, for lack of a better term, but their disagreements may cause their use of the power to be unstable, and therefore even more dangerous. Our task is to restore the balance that the Kavanaghs have disrupted, and that could cause wider problems."

"Like what?" Darrick asked.

"Lourana has told me how they consume people, and what they did to the river. That could be only a start. They have the power to destroy human life and damage water, that much we know, but what of the other elements? Earth and air, the green world?"

Darrick thought this druid had way more questions than he had answers. It was clear there was really just one answer. He had to kill the Kavanaghs, all of them, if he could. Without mercy, and rid the world of this unholy thing.

"You've been intent on killing one another," Cathbad said, as if he'd read his thoughts. "That's not a satisfactory end."

"One or the other of us has to win. I intend it to be me." He glanced sidelong at Lourana, and she gave his hand a little squeeze.

The druid took another sip of tea. He was a cool customer, Darrick had to give him that.

"I don't think you alone are strong enough to win, not even though you did before, as Lourana has told me."

"Not alone. Lourana saved me."

"She's rather modest on that point."

Darrick saw her blushing and thought, *you look shy as a girl but I know you're a warrior.*

"I brought you together with Rory once so that I could learn what you each are. I want to bring you together again to negotiate, but you must use restraint and not allow yourself to be goaded into a response. Lourana has agreed to mediate."

"I wasn't well pleased to go along with this," Lourana said, "but I don't see any other way. We can't run from them forever."

"He's hypnotized you, affected your mind!" Darrick turned to face her. "What does he know of what we've been through?"

"He knows. All of it. And he's spoken with Rory, who wants to be free of the others, get them out of his head."

"You're relying on Rory? Whoever he is, however much of him is his father? You taught me what the Kavanaghs are, and now you'd trust them?" He took both her hands, leaned closer. She didn't avoid his direct gaze. *Thank God I'm not sensing fear. She's not flinching away any longer.*

"Rory is being tormented by Eamon, as he has been his whole life, but from within now," Cathbad said. "The father's personality is strong, strongest, but Rory resists. As does Cormac."

He ignored the druid and focused on Lourana. "You cannot want to do this."

"Darrick, I don't *want* any of this, but it came to my door and now I have to see it through. You'd do nothing different if the shoe was on the other foot."

"And you trust him? Cathbad?"

"I do." Her voice was almost fervent. "I stood face to face with the Kavanaghs, the whole kit and caboodle, and my life wouldn't have been worth a thin dime except Cathbad and his people encircled us with light or power or something. They couldn't reach me."

Darrick spent a long moment searching her face, searching himself to test what was happening between them. He wanted to know where she'd been, how Cathbad had talked her into this, but realized it was really just jealousy talking. *Lourana trusted me when I was a horrible creature. I have to trust her now.*

He turned to Cathbad. "She claims you have power, that you can command nature. How?"

"Not command," he said solemnly. "That's where we've gone wrong. Conquering. Traumatizing."

Darrick motioned impatiently. "All right, all right. But where does this come from?"

"I've inherited a ragged mantle, I'll admit. Fragments written down long after the druids were dust. The Orders of today were built on these fragments, and intuitions, and sometimes pure romance. When the Romans drove the British druids into extinction on Anglesey, we of Ireland melted into the populace and the desolate places, avoiding the authorities and the burning pyres. For all their Christianity, the Irish are Celtic Christians, which means they've not lost touch with the earth and its forces."

It all sounded too much like the kind of people who claimed to be able to visit past lives or do astral projection. "I don't sense anything like the Kavanaghs, or myself, in you."

"And you wouldn't." Cathbad downed the last of his cold tea. "Druids are not about exerting force to rule over others. We are first of all poets. We see the world in metaphor, which is simply the relation of one thing to another, and strive to restore the proper balance."

"I know Cormac is a poet." Lourana thought about the slender young man leaning against the massive mantelpiece at Knockaulin House, a book of poetry in his hand. "Is that why he's helping Rory?

"I've only had a bit of contact with him, I fear, thanks to Eamon's dominance, but such inclination can only be helpful."

"I'm lost," Darrick admitted.

"We are the devotees of Brighid, the goddess of poets and source of wisdom. She's also the protector of the people and the land. We call upon her powers that come from the living earth."

Darrick had a bad feeling about all this storybook stuff. Poets. Goddesses! He'd keep his peace, however, and rely only upon himself when the moment came. That's all he could rely on. The druid might at least provide a distraction with his incantations, while he tried to end the Kavanaghs.

"So where is Rory? You're in touch with him, I guess."

"I am. They are for now focused on tracking down their ancestry — like you, Darrick, they are unsatisfied with what they know of their past."

Lourana spoke up. "Pap always said a man that's proud of his ancestors is like a potato. The best part of him is in the ground."

Cathbad guffawed. "A wise man, your pap."

Darrick had no patience for this. Not with the Kavanaghs lurking. "You know their true origins?"

"That I do not. They claim the lineage of Leinster, and boast the crest of the kings with great assurance, but I am doubtful."

Darrick remembered Eamon bragging about the carved shield with the lions, the symbol of some ancient family. They were predators, like their lions, and he thought it sounded dangerous to offer something to a deadly creature that you weren't assured of giving.

"We have a difficult passage ahead, and I cannot guarantee what the outcome will be," Cathbad said. "But if the matter is not brought to the test, it will go worse for you, them, and maybe much more."

Darrick shook his head. It sounded like a slow-motion disaster.

"And you, Darrick. You are troubled by the mysterious circumstance of your birth, how that may be connected to your sudden power. I haven't forgotten."

Now Darrick gave a little laugh. "You'd have to be a wizard to learn any more than I have. The records are drowned and no one's left to ask."

Cathbad nodded. "It may be so."

"More tea?" Lourana asked as she switched on the kettle. She might have been back in her own little kitchen, on the edge of a dark pine forest in West Virginia. They both said yes to another cup, knowing there were hard issues to be discussed, now that they'd agreed on this course.

As Darrick waited for the kettle to boil, he asked Lourana what had been on his mind all the while.

"About an hour ago, I heard you speak. You said you were on the way."

She looked startled. "Heard me?"

"In my mind. I thought I was hallucinating, but it was as though you were right here as you are now, this close."

"I remember thinking that," she said. "I was so eager to see you."

Cathbad's mouth pursed, then relaxed. "There's more to Lourana, too, it seems."

Chapter 34

It was the auspicious day, according to the druid, but not because of the weather. Rory had left in the early dark, in rain driven by a swirling wind. The drops hammered against the windshield, then let off, only to come again from the side on a powerful gust. As he approached Cnoc Ailinne, he could see lights on in the farmhouse and barn as the family went about its routine, weather or no. The gate was open for him. He parked beside a flimsy-looking car, the druid's he imagined. He pulled on the Barbour waterproof and cinched down the hood before opening the door into a cold blast that soaked his face.

Welcome to Ireland. Padraig.

He walked up the hill by flashlight, the path bubbling away in rivulets under his feet. As he neared the top, he saw a circle of light from a lantern, and Cathbad in a long coat. The soaked hem of his robe flapped around his ankles.

Cannot trust him. Eamon.

We need him, Domnall counseled.

When we have our own. No giving way to druid or brehon.

Eamon was raising a gale to match the deluge. *Kings powerful as Cú Chulainn.*

Am I the only one who's not delusional, Rory wondered.

The day was beginning to arrive, but it was a slow dawn, a gradual lightening with no glimpse of sun through impenetrable clouds. The druid kept consulting his watch, the blue flash like a lightning-bug in the gloom.

"As dawn arrives, you must stand on this stone," Cathbad said, his voice raised against the wind. "The footprint stone has been lost, but this is part of the Ail, the great marker-stone, as ancient and as holy. It can bear witness."

Rory stepped close to the slab, tested it with one foot. It rocked a little and squelched in the sodden turf.

"Did not Jesus say the very stones would speak truth? Here in Ireland the stones give voice to recognize a king. The Lia Fáil, which was stolen away to Scotland and then England, was but one of many. Here at Dún Ailinne for the kingdom of Leinster, as at the others, the king places a foot on the coronation stone of his realm, pledging himself to the land and people, and a rightful king is made known."

The sky was a little bit brighter. Rory and Cathbad huddled against the wind as it swirled, now from one side, then 90 degrees away and back. The druid checked his watch again.

"Now."

Rory stepped up onto the slick stone. He heard the wind only, shrieking as the stone was supposed to do.

"Do you claim the lineage of the Kavanagh, last kings of Leinster?"

"I do."

"Do you assert your blood bond to this land and people?"

"I do."

There is no outcry. Eamon.

No song. Cormac.

A memory came of Darrick taunting Eamon, "Anyone with a horse and a couple of cows was a king in Ireland." Rory shifted his feet and looked at Cathbad, who was again checking his watch.

"Let the true king be acclaimed!"

No sound.

He invoked for the second time, and a third, and was answered by the same silence.

Dawn definitely had arrived; despite the heavy clouds, the light could be seen spreading. The attempt had failed.

Eamon muscled to the top of the clamor, forced his way through Rory's throat.

"You've deceived us," he rumbled.

Cathbad edged away. "I promised you the time and place, the opportunity and nothing more. If the stone fails to speak, that's perhaps the lack of the footprint stone itself."

"You said this stone was sufficient."

"I did. But many centuries have passed."

"And the stone forgets?"

"Or the lineage has been broken."

Rory shuddered with Eamon's rage at the druid's doubt, at how he had been suppressed at Kildare, at this man who had knowledge and power yet could not or would not bring about the desired confirmation.

"You aid Darrick. You prevented us from taking Lourana."

Then Padraig, who had been only a rudimentary presence when Rory first inherited his terrible legacy, forced his way past Eamon.

This is a fool's venture. The Kavanaghs are not kings, that I know, and sure we are not from a poet who sired naught but words.

Rory had stepped down from the stone and sat huddled with his back to the blast, unable to trust his body as Eamon's anger grew and the collective shifted within.

You'll hear me now, my lads.

Padraig had been getting stronger since the day they landed in Dublin, and Rory had felt his rough presence more and more whenever Eamon faded. His only respite from the fathers had been retreat into that corner of his mind where Cormac too was finding refuge.

You've looked into the Shannon Pot. Fools blather it's bottomless, that a woman drowned for its secret, but that water flows from the mountain like any river. It has a true source. We Kavanaghs have a true source.

The others protested, *where, what, how could that have been obscured?* Eamon shouted of the line of kings. Padraig's son Domnall admitted that when he gained his father's spirit, that was when he learned of their origins.

And you heeded me. You did not allow my bones to rot in the dirt. You kept counsel and built our proper crypt in the bosom of the coal.

Rory tried to assert himself. He lifted his head, threw back his hood to let the rain wash over him, and found that Cathbad was now very close, his open hands lifted above Rory's dripping head in a sort of blessing, but he could feel nothing but the grating of Padraig on his spirit.

Deep under Ireland's soil is a power older than kings, older than the gods. I will take you there.

Eamon cried, *Then we need no deceiving magician!* Eamon forced Rory's body into action and extended his hand toward the druid, who had lowered his own benediction, if that was what it was, but did not cower from the threat.

Compelled by Eamon and the others to feed, Rory touched the druid's shoulder and waited for the glow of life to begin streaming into him. Instead, he saw that green-gold illumination take shape. It felt clean but also intimidating, like powerful surf, like an ancient forest moss-deep with its own secrets.

"You'll find I am a tough old tree, you Kavanaghs."

They remembered the attack on Darrick, how that man had turned his father's rage back upon himself inside the crypt Domnall used to bury the family secret. This resistance was different.

"I call upon Brighid, protector, to bar this corrupt power, to place around me the hedge no man can cross."

Eamon raged against the druid, against Rory for his failures, against his broken hopes. Finally, he fell into incoherence. He let Rory reclaim his body.

We'll have our way with the druid yet. Padraig.

With them all. Eamon.

As Rory watched, a heavy fog gathered out of the rain and cloaked the druid, then blotted out the whole top of the hill. When he could see again, the sky was bright, and Cathbad was no longer there.

Chapter 35

Cathbad had left without saying where he was going, or when he'd be back. Darrick gave him a long dark stare as he opened the door and went out. Lourana felt a little bereft though she certainly wouldn't tell Darrick that. She'd found comfort in the druid's presence.

First thing though, with him away, Lourana plugged in her phone to charge and called Dreama.

"Oh Momma, I've tried and tried to call! What's wrong?"

"I lost my cord and ran out of power," she said, and saw Darrick give her a look. "That's all."

"That's just silly. Doesn't Darrick have one?"

"He has an Apple. Mine's an Android. We don't fit."

"Then don't be so cheap — go buy one."

"You're right, baby. How are you?"

"I'm fine, working. What about you?"

"Just being tourists, going to see the Blarney Stone and that sort of thing. I did the thing with bending back and kissing it." Lourana marveled at her newfound ability to make up stuff on the fly. "I saw shamrocks growing all wild in the woods, just like you'd see dandelions back home."

"So now I'll have to watch out for your silver tongue."

Lourana felt a pang, as though Dreama had somehow known that her story was far from the truth.

Neither one of them mentioned Rory. Dreama knew where her mother stood, and Lourana — well, she no longer knew where she stood. It was, as they say, complicated. She'd not told Darrick.

They'd resumed their temporary life in Killeshandra but couldn't feel easy, wondering when Cathbad would reappear. Lourana didn't want to look beyond that. Perhaps it would work out, this negotiation, and they'd go their separate ways.

At their familiar pub, the waitress beamed at seeing Lourana back with Darrick, "And all's well," she declared.

They ordered a big meal and ate with gusto, aware that food tasted good for the first time in some days.

That evening, Lourana outlined her adventures with the druid, which seemed almost like a fairy tale even as she told the literal truth. The cottage hidden in the deep woods, and a townhouse in Kildare. The forest in flower, the fire circle, Brighid's house, the meeting with Rory. It was all just one click past real. Maybe two.

Darrick, on the other hand, had little to report. Waiting, that's what he'd done.

"I did do something out of character," he admitted.

"What was that?"

"I went to church."

"I thought you didn't observe."

"I don't. Or didn't. But I stayed for the Mass."

"Was it — good?"

He shrugged. "I can't say. I just felt this desire, when I passed this church as I was driving around, and I turned and went back. It was St. Brigid's."

"Of course."

He smiled. "It's that or St. Patrick's, right?"

"So did you do the whole thing, confession, and all that?"

"No. I did not." The flash of humor was gone as he turned somber. "I am in mortal sin, but I didn't want to make my confession, didn't know how I could explain, therefore I could not take the Sacrament."

"I don't think it's some kind of mortal sin that you killed in self-defense, and to save others."

"Not the first time, no. That was a surprise, an accident. Maybe not the second, when I was aware but couldn't control it. But I killed that loathsome newspaper editor with full intention, Lourana. Even to protect you, it was still murder, nothing less. I don't need a priest to tell me that."

Lourana didn't know about all this Catholic stuff, but she'd known all along how much the deaths had weighed on him. Seemed like the church visit hadn't done him any good. Maybe harm.

The discussion seemed to plunge Darrick into gloom, as though something demanded that his happiness at her return had to be balanced with despair. He plowed into his books, reading like he was cramming for a test. Lourana was roused from half-sleep by him reading out a passage.

". . . a witch will cut a hand from a corpse, and enchanting it, 'will stir a well and skim from its surface a neighbor's butter.' That's what it says. Also, a candle placed in the fingers of a dead hand can't be extinguished. Criminals carry a dead hand to have a source of light for their deeds."

"What is that you're reading? Makes me think of those old ghost stories from back home."

"Yeats. The poet. Well, his collection of fairy tales and legends." He showed her the cover. "Amazing, bizarre stuff. Listen to this: A black cat's liver can be dried and ground up to make a love potion to put into someone's tea. It must be poured from a black teapot to work."

"Of course."

"Maybe your druid friend added something to our tea."

"Don't scoff til we get through this."

"All right."

"And talk to me about something that's not dead hands and such."

He looked at her with tenderness, as though he realized and regretted how he'd brought up memories she was trying to forget. About being forced into the black room. Before the light had been turned off, and there was only the illusion of lights moving in complete darkness, she had seen Dreama reach out to put her hand on Cormac's. All that was left of it, just bones.

Chapter 36

It came back to the coal. Again.

Rory once thought he'd be able to leave that all behind in West Virginia, find a new career far from the bleak landscape of the coal-fields, but his father's death had bound him to the remains of KCL. The rotting albatross around his neck. The company was coming apart but not in the way his father had planned. Still, it stayed alive, and ever more problematic from the messages he was avoiding. Like a zombie, he thought, and Eamon was amused. *That's what they called Darrick.*

Even as he drove north, his mind retreated into that narrow space where he could sometimes exist apart from his father. Cormac said it was the place of poetry, therefore the literalists could not enter. Perhaps. Rory had welcomed him into his "escape room," and maybe he couldn't have found it himself except for the presence of Cormac's poetic sensibility. Still, as much as Rory needed an ally, he was beginning to feel that Cormac's literary passions and his desire for Dreama were coloring his inmost being.

Padraig, whose presence he'd barely registered before, was now the strongest of all but Eamon, who sulked in his fury at the druid's failure and Padraig's claims about the common roots of the family. *No kingship, but the kinship of the coal face,* he said. *We must get down to the coal.* So they were going to County Roscommon, to the re-created coal mine of the Arigna Experience, *as close as you'll now get to the source.* They had left Cathbad, disgraced, out of their plans. Padraig said this was no place for the late-come gods, those faded fairy folk the druid trafficked with, much less the foreign arrivals such as Jesus from Nazareth.

Dimly, Rory was aware that Padraig was reacting to a familiar landscape as it passed, spotting traces of the mining past in rough hills where trees had rooted into the slag of iron mines and coal mines, hollows that marked old workings, brick buildings abandoned and others repurposed. Rory thought that somewhere in that landscape, acid was leaching from the coal as it had in West Virginia. As his family had manipulated such mine drainage to poison the river in pursuit of corporate strategy.

The tourist mine was marked by two ultramodern slant-faced buildings of glass and steel that reminded Rory more of Pei's pyramids than the spoil heaps they were supposed to emulate. It was early, more than two hours before scheduled opening time, but the operators were eager to host the leader of a major American coal company who had an interest in supporting their project. The family had ancestors who had worked in the mines of Ireland, Brodie had informed them as he arranged the private tour. Even at long distance, Brodie was as always devoted to the family's needs.

The tour guide, an elderly board member who'd lived all his life in the valley, fitted Rory with a white helmet and the requisite safety lecture.

"You'll find the access remarkably easy, as the beds are near to the surface, not like your deep mines in the States," he said, as they entered along a wheelchair-accessible corridor. "Easy in but not easy out — the miners worked with short shovels and picks, on their backs or sides, to chip away at the thin seams."

He pointed out the structure of the mine, "which you'll be no doubt familiar with," the main tunnel with adits driven into the seams.

Rory didn't tell him that he'd never been down in even one of the KCL mines, now his mines. Unlike his father, grandfather, and before. Once he remembered telling his father that his hands would never be blackened, and getting slapped hard for his impudence. Hard enough that he fell, being only 10 or 11, and slight at that, his father looming over him red-faced as though he would kill him on the spot.

The guide drew his attention to the sound of water dripping. "A recording only, for the sake of realism, but the men actually worked in water, soaked through as they dug. But we were lucky here. The mines kept most of this valley from starving when the Hunger came."

They reached the naked coal, and here the guide excused himself with fulsome assurances of how interested the board was to hear about how KCL wanted to be involved, and that a small reception was being laid on, following this private time for the Kavanagh heir to commune with the foundation of his fortune.

Crow coal, whispered Padraig.

Look at the shine on its feathers. Cormac.

In western Virginia, I found seams so high a man could work like a man and not grovel. But it was these mines prepared me to rise in the new world.

Rory thought, he means the rigors of mining here. That gave him the necessary fortitude and will.

Put your hands on the coal, Rory. I'll not call you by my name til you prove yourself worthy of it. Lay your hands to the coal and see.

Reluctantly, he put one palm to the coal face.

Don't be a coward. Eamon.

Rory knew, however, that his father likewise did not understand why Padraig had brought them there. He placed his other palm against the black stone. It was cool and felt a bit damp. A fragment loosened and fell at his feet. With the atmospheric dim light and the fake sound of water, Rory felt more than a little foolish to continue with this bit of theater. He began to back away, but felt himself pulled forward and slammed to the wall of coal, his face forced against it, his heart thumping against it.

Then he saw.

With his eye pressed close to the coal, what should be utter blackness, he saw a moving shape. A being showed itself in the coal, blackness within blackness. It was not his father's will that had pushed him forward but this creature that had pulled him bodily to the wall. He shuddered at the apparition, something like a man with the head of a goat and one staring eye.

Satan, he thought.

They were here before Satan was hatched.

Dimly, Rory could see others gathering behind. Some were missing a leg, or an arm, or had a human face disfigured. Black shapes moved inside the coal like fish swirling in water. The cool dampness was the touch of their bodies, and if he could have wrenched himself away even at the loss of his own flesh, he would have.

These are the Fomóraigh. When I delved black coal to feed the Irish smelter and the English furnace, they were there, rulers of the nether world from as long ago as the earth was made.

Rory was battered by the chaos they represented, the primeval call to destruction, as the creatures reached wordlessly into his thoughts, sent dark threads spinning through his body.

They took hold of me, down in the depths where no man was near to help nor prayer to save, and I was afraid. But I was not emptied of life but filled. As coal is made from the sun, boggy peat drawing up in darkness to make something greater, they taught me how to take the sun of life from others.

The strangeness of Rory's own cluttered spirit, and the unknown that was Darrick, paled beside these creatures.

We need fear no more from brehon or druid. They draw their powers from the Tuatha Dé, and that light is no longer strong enough to stand against us.

Chapter 37

Rory ran himself to exhaustion that afternoon. The rain was unrelenting and he was glad of it, welcomed the cold gale roaring with ice in its teeth off the North Atlantic. From the hotel out to Howth Head and around that hilly peninsula, battered by the wind, he pounded through the wet until he stood bent double with hands on thighs, trembling. Now he could sleep, surely.

But a hot shower that sluiced the muck from his legs could do nothing for his mind. The luxurious bed held no attraction, because as soon as he began to drift off, the monstrous figures in the coal came swirling into his thoughts.

This was always the source, Padraig reminded, full of his ascendancy. *How could I have prospered in a new world, alone and friendless, but that I carried this with me? They guided me to riches underground.*

The others muttered.

You children. Thought you'd done it all on your own. You've none of you known the brute work I did. Now my sons do their delving in land books.

You might have kept this to yourself, Rory answered.

Eamon? You have your answer.

No response from the others. Domnall knew the secret and did not pass it on. Others were as shocked as Rory was, now able to recognize the Fomóraigh threading within them all. He could picture the elaborate family tree going up in smoke, tossed on the hearth-fire below the carved symbols of royalty. Knockaulin House was built on a lie. In some ways it was a relief to have Eamon silenced with his fantasies of royal blood, but not by the introduction of the repulsive shape and sense of those beings. Rory could trace, now, how they'd always been there, the black ribbon twisting through his thoughts, sending him into depressions where he lashed out at friends. And what would happen when he met with Darrick? How could any truce succeed? The druid was a pathetic figure to stand against such ancient darkness, and he could sense in the Fomóraigh an eagerness to face, and destroy, Darrick. Not because of his threat. Just because destruction was their nature.

His thoughts spun until finally, he called Dreama.

She must have been anticipating his call, because she was made up, her black hair brushed to gleaming (that sheen of the coal) and the necklace that Cormac had given her was clasped around her throat.

"Hi."

"Hello, Dreama. You look lovely."

"Thank you." Her dimple deepened as she bent her head a bit. "It's good to see you — but your face looks all red."

"I was running in the wind. And the rain."

"That doesn't sound very pleasant. I don't think Cormac ever liked to do such things. Did you?"

Cormac sighed in his thoughts.

"Cormac?"

"Yes, Dreama, I'm here." Rory didn't struggle as Cormac came to the fore. "You're right, I'd prefer a warm fire and a good book."

"I'd be curled up close to you," she purred.

The memory of just such a night, a fire roaring in the library, Cormac sitting on the deep couch with his pen and journal, and Dreama in a turquoise silk slip nestled into his side, her legs under a fluffy coverlet.

Rory's body stirred, an unwilled erection that was all Cormac.

"When are you coming home?"

"I'm not sure," he said curtly, fighting the sensual glow that was pouring through him.

"Aren't things going well?"

"You could say that."

"Grumpy man." He saw her lips form a pout.

Cormac was everywhere, his thoughts rich with phrases as he described Dreama's body to himself, writing the reality of it within Rory's flesh. He was kissing her, taking her tongue lightly between his teeth, running his hand down her thigh and then across her mons, teasing her with his fingers so that her hips rose to seek him. Rory's erection was almost painful as Cormac remembered pulling her over atop him, entering her sharply as she gasped, getting lost in the warm depths of her.

Rory climaxed, pulsing with Cormac's need.

"Let me go," he hissed aloud.

"What?" Dreama answered.

Cormac offered apology, but Rory was enraged now, lashing out at his uncle, forcing him out of his refuge.

"Cormac? Rory?"

"Can't talk now," he managed.

He clicked and threw the phone across the room, satisfied to hear it slam against a table. His thoughts swirled darkly.

The Fomóraigh. As his violent anger ebbed, he realized where it had come from. He thought about his father's rages and wondered how often those were truly him, and how much the creatures that Padraig had welcomed into himself and his heirs.

Cormac was his only ally and he'd pushed him away, unable to cope with ceding his self not only to his father but now his uncle as well.

Rory was disgusted by his body's betrayal, semen sticky on his thighs, and his mind's betrayal. And not a soul he could talk to.

Chapter 38

Lourana had spent much of the night reassuring Darrick about this course of action, letting him talk out all the pros and cons. Nothing new, just the same tired circling, led by their anxiety around and around. Like a pony ride at the carnival, the poor beasts tied to a creaking wheel.

Cathbad had arrived early at their Kildare lodgings, dressed like the middle-aged teacher he was, thankfully with no evidence of pagan regalia. "And now we'll see," he said as they pulled up to the meeting site an hour later. He lagged behind, and when Lourana looked back, she saw him taking his staff from the back. *So much for the 21st century.*

The meeting had been set for a neutral space, Cathbad forging an agreement for an "interested parties" visit to a former whiskey aging warehouse at the outskirts of the city. A keypad let them enter the cavernous space still fragrant from barrels that had rested here for years of mellowing. Swallows twittered high above, swooping in and out of ventilation grates. After a little while, they heard the electronic buzz of the lock, and moved to the opposite side as Rory entered.

Darrick glanced over at her, his gray eyes made strange by the lenses of his glasses. She saw Cathbad pass him the car keys. That alarmed her. *What did they say when I wasn't around?*

Rory came partway across the floor and Darrick did the same, while she stayed near an exit. She thought he looked even worse than Darrick, his face raw and windburned, with bags under his eyes.

Cathbad stood between them. He raised his staff, clutching it with both hands. "In the name of Brighid, bringer of concord, I ask you to speak honestly but with restraint."

"I want. . ." Rory began, and then his lips twisted and pressed together.

"We want peace," Darrick said. "But we need assurances that the Kavanaghs will hound us no more."

"I agree," Rory said, with difficulty.

Lourana took note that he said "I" and not "we." Did the other Kavanaghs go along with this? She remembered that old line about "trust but verify," and wondered how on earth they thought to accomplish that. She could tell that the young Kavanagh was struggling with the ancestors jumbled up inside him, as his expression and even the movement of his body changed. Right now, she was sure that Eamon was in charge, by his glowering brow and the wide stance that indicated a far more massive figure.

"Ancestors, speak," said Cathbad, and he lowered his staff.

Eamon immediately came forward. "We demand security," he said, his voice like rocks tumbling down a chute.

Then Rory's body eased, and the familiar tones of his uncle came through: "We want to reach agreement."

Lourana recognized the whispered voice of Patrick, confirming, and Rory's body showed the hunched immobility of the old man she'd seen filling a huge chair.

This was all going according to plan. Too much so.

There was a pause. She heard other voices, sullen or harsh, new to her, claiming their desire for peace from what seemed like a great distance.

Rory's body shook.

Eamon was back. "And where does this peacemaking leave us? I have no assurance from you," he accused Darrick.

"I was not the aggressor," he replied.

"You destroyed me. I cannot let that happen again."

Lourana saw Darrick's back stiffen, the way he seemed to lean forward, and she expected at any minute to see Rory begin to show the effects.

"Darrick, don't become what they are," she cried.

"We cannot trust them."

"We cannot trust you."

Hasn't it ever been the case, Lourana thought. *Men have to win every battle.*

Cathbad tried to reclaim the dialog by raising his staff and invoking a veil of light between the enemies. Both men moved back a step from the glowing barrier and seemed to relax, relent.

It seemed like that might be the end of it, Cathbad halting the back and forth, the sides locked in their positions. A wasted effort. Then Rory's eyes grew wide and he fell hard, hitting his head and convulsing on the concrete. Lourana was moving to help him when she saw a shadow rise from his body.

"I am Padraig," came a harsh voice with an Irish accent. "I began the dynasty."

But the figure that appeared above Rory's limp form was not human.

Cathbad was closest to this gathering shape. He did not retreat but stayed within the barrier of light he'd summoned as the shadow thickened, swirled, took form as a sort of misshapen version of a human, but with an animal's head and only one hoofed leg and one clawed hand. It remained something not quite solid, shifting to another kind of half-completed being, missing one part or another. A single staring eye glowed within the shadow and then faded away.

"Brighid, shield the world from this undoing!" His voice shook.

Padraig spoke again, or something did. The unspoken words came from the monstrous figure rather than Rory's unconscious form. "We are older than your Tree-Queen. Our power is greater." A brutal burst of something like Gaelic made Cathbad go pale and flinch, but he held fast.

"Go," he said to Lourana, his voice strained to breaking.

She opened the door but didn't leave. The shadow advanced on the druid and his light ebbed, twilight as night came sweeping over the bright world and plunging it into darkness.

Then Darrick was moving to stand beside the druid, inside that leaf-hued glory, and Lourana realized he was exerting himself against the creature, pushing it away from them and back toward Rory.

The shadow rotated, swung from side to side, and abruptly was gone, plunging back inside Rory.

"Darrick, Lourana, go now."

The young man looked dead. Lourana wavered, but Darrick grabbed her hand and pulled her outside.

"I will meet you in Kildare!" Cathbad called after them.

And they were out under a clearing sky. Swallows dipped and the river flashed at Lourana as she gulped for clean air.

Chapter 39

Darrick was driving too fast, gripping the wheel with white knuckles, but Lourana wasn't about to say anything. She might have driven even faster, to get away from whatever the hell that was. They went back to the rented house and crawled under the covers like children terrified of thunder and lightning, arms wrapped around each other, her head buried into his shoulder. But then, was there any rational adult way to deal with what had just happened?

They didn't talk. The encounter seemed to have drained them of words.

By late afternoon, roused by hunger, they went out for a quick bite, but felt exposed and soon hurried back. After dark, a knock at the door. She got up and peeked through the gap between the curtain and the wall and saw Cathbad in the glare of a streetlight, in front of a van gaudily painted with shamrocks.

"Should I let him in?"

"Is he alone?"

"As far as I can tell." She watched as Cathbad came to knock again. He looked haggard, almost shrunken. She waited, then as he walked away, turned the lock and opened the door a crack.

"No Rory?"

He shook his head. After a moment, she opened the door and he jogged back and slipped inside.

"You knew it was going to go bad!" All the anger she had pent up from the confrontation was boiling to come out and she didn't hold back. "I saw you give Darrick the car keys so we could get away. You *knew*."

"I didn't know, but it's best to be prepared."

"We weren't."

"No, not for that." He backed away from the anger that had her leaning forward, but he didn't sit down.

"What was *that thing*?" Darrick roused himself from whatever internal place he'd been. "That was not like the Kavanaghs were before. And I would know."

Cathbad clasped his hands as though he might start trembling. "I recognize what it is, but never before have I confronted the Fomóraigh."

"It's demonic," Darrick said.

"Better to consider it — them, because they are many — as an ancient race, evil to our eyes but truly primeval, only half formed. They existed before the gods I serve, spawned out of chaos. They were keepers of the deep places of the earth and under the sea."

Darrick raised his head. "So are they stronger than your Brighid?"

"They were vanquished by her and the other Tuatha Dé Danaan in the morning of the world." He paused. "They are — other. I did not know they still interacted with the living. Or even that they existed. How the Kavanaghs came in contact with them, I don't know."

"They felt foul," Lourana said.

"To use metaphor, as I do, you might think of water. Clean water, dirty water. The Fomóraigh represent all that is gross, heavy, and dark, that sinks to the bottom, while Brighid is keeper of clean water, the wells and pools that are the womb of life, and mist and fog that mediate between earth and sky."

"I thought you said she was about fire," Lourana put in.

"She is many things. Also the moon. Precognition."

"We could have used some of that precognition, now couldn't we?" Darrick sneered.

Cathbad pulled himself up from his exhausted slump. "I am merely a devotee. I don't demand. We will return to the fire temple and ask Brighid's direct intercession against her ancient adversaries. We need every bit of power we can muster if we face them again."

"As we will," said Darrick.

Cathbad looked closely at him. "Thank you for daring to come within the light and stand beside me."

Darrick seemed to turn that over before he spoke. "It seemed like, maybe it was the right thing, but I don't understand what happened."

"Brighid's light allowed us to push the dark ones back. I always suspected the Kavanaghs were delusional about their ancestry, but was willing to give them a path — and yes, I was an opportunist, because I thought I could turn their pride into support for our efforts. We make those kinds of accommodations sometimes." Lourana saw a spark in his eyes again, something of that cunning leprechaun glint. "They did not accomplish the link with the past they expected, and they're not pleased with me as a result, but I expected to offer them something that would satisfy. Then this happened."

"Sounds like you miscalculated." *Might as well say it, since he can read my mind.*

"I have been known to do that. But I did learn much, mostly about Darrick. I was disbelieving of your power, then suspicious of it, if it had anything to do with our people and our land. But when you slipped inside Brighid's fire with ease, then I was sure you'd inherited something ancient. Ancient and good."

"That brehon thing? How?"

"We are all haunted by our ancestors, right? It's called DNA. Because Irish druids remained among the people, resisting Rome, the teachings continued generation to generation — and so did the powers." His right hand found the amulet and pressed it against his chest. "I have some small access to the powers of druids through my own family's long history. And you are indeed linked to the hereditary arbiters who maintained the bounds of Celtic society. It took a crisis to awaken your gift."

"Curse."

This talk of inheritance and power reminded Lourana way too much of the Kavanaghs.

"Unlike the Kavanaghs," the druid said. "Their power does not rise out of their humanity."

Darrick asked about Rory, if he still lived, and Lourana was a bit surprised at that. She had learned how Darrick avoided emotional pain through routine and solitude, protecting himself from the rough edges of the world, until this new power was awakened. His responses were triggered by violent emotion, and he was exquisitely sensitive to the mental states of others, but he had never before shown empathy for their opponents.

"He's alive, all too alive some might say. Direct access to the Fomóraigh has given the Kavanaghs an infusion of dark energy. Rory himself has suffered, however."

Darrick nodded.

"His mind was attacked and his physical body, until he was all but comatose. I stayed with him and helped him climb back to consciousness."

"Because you're as much for them as for us," Lourana said. She couldn't help herself, anger simmering now to sarcasm.She thought about how Cathbad had tracked them. The surprise at the church. Then she considered Darrick and tried to put a lid on her nasty self.

"Because of compassion. He is a living being, a human being, however possessed. It was a near thing, if he would come back to himself, or if Padraig or Eamon would take complete control. I guided his spirit back and got him to his hotel to recover."

She realized how much of a risk he had taken. She caught Darrick's eye and saw the same realization there.

"In that time, I learned that Rory is genuine about seeking peace, even to the point of sacrificing himself. I think he would die before becoming Padraig's puppet, if he has the possibility of choosing."

"Why is Rory different from the rest?" asked Darrick.

"Every human being is a balance, male and female elements. We tilt one way or the other. And so with Rory. But the old Kavanaghs, it's as though they expunged all that is female from themselves. They are hypermasculine, violent. The presence of the Fomóraigh, I believe, lies at the root of their unbalance."

"But how is he worth saving?" insisted Lourana.

"How are any of us worth saving?" She felt like a student, suitably chastised. "He — and Cormac as well — perhaps acquired a stronger genetic component from their mothers. They are more equitable, more human if you will, and so the Fomóraigh are especially damaging to them, now that they have fully emerged. In time, exposed to that presence, I expect Rory will become like his forefathers."

"What comes next?" Darrick asked.

"I honestly don't know. We'll get some rest and then on the morrow do what we can to be better prepared for that next thing."

Chapter 40

Cathbad opened the door to leave, and the Kavanaghs stood in his way. Rory pushed into the room, or Rory's body anyway, moving Cathbad aside like a man made of air.

Darrick could feel the energy pulsing through that slender form and it felt of Eamon's crushing dominance and Padraig's brutality. He moved back, trying to shield Lourana, as Rory slammed shut the door and a sinuous black form sifted from his body and took shape around him. Something that resembled a tail flicked out and then disappeared. One red eye appeared, then two, then none. He was embraced by the creature, his outline blurring as though he were merging with it.

"We want what is ours," came the voice from Rory's throat, but it was not human. Darrick realized that what they wanted was the whole earth.

"This is not your place. Go back to the depths for which you were made," said Cathbad.

"They took me as one of their own," and now the voice was Padraig's, or mostly. "Down in the coal, they taught me to take life from the living."

The black form swirled.

"Fomóraigh, ancient ones, you were defeated by the Tuatha Dé before, and you will be again. Leave this man's body and depart from the living lands. We invoke the light of Brighid."

Darrick could almost see the druid's words fall to dust and blow away. Something shook him like a chew toy and flung him into the corner.

He searched for an emotional lever he could push against. *The druid confirmed my power comes from good.* He tested an opening and was bludgeoned by the bottomless envy that the dark has for the light, the subterranean for those allowed to walk in the light, rivers plunged underground for the bright waters that sparkle in the sun.

He pushed with all his being.

Rory, or whatever that was, smiled, unfazed, and slammed his psychic energy back against him.

Darrick staggered, was lifted to be flung into the bedroom, help-less. He was sinking. The light around him was becoming blue.

He heard Lourana cry out and he tried to answer but he wasn't really there any longer.

Memory flashes. Holy water dripping from his fingers. Flickering candles. A sense of deep peace he hadn't known he missed.

The light around him shaded to purple, then it was not light any longer, as what remained of his awareness spiraled slowly down to the abyss.

A figure of mercy showed herself. A woman with a kind face and open arms extended to accept his broken self.

Lourana?

Brighid?

He gave himself to the figure.

Mary full of grace be with me.

Mother?

He heard a clear carrying whistle, like a dying swan.

Then it was all white light, the light they'd always promised would be there.

Chapter 41

Lourana watched horrified as Cathbad crumpled awkwardly against the wall and lay motionless, and Darrick, *oh Darrick,* was lifted from his feet and tossed onto the bed, slack, apparently not breathing.

I can't help them.

The Kavanaghs turned their attention to her.

She was so alone. The room seemed far too small to hold all this, the discarded men, dead it seemed, the creature that enclosed Rory manifesting claws and eyes and behind it all the time, a painting of a girl picking flowers.

Nothing ventured.

"Rory, I know you're there."

She thought she saw a flash of recognition in his eyes, and momentarily his body seemed to become more his, and less the dark thing that moved around him.

"Rory, you have to help. Fight it. Remember Dreama. Cormac, think about Dreama."

The darkness shifted, and with it, the Kavanaghs flowed through and across Rory's face. At any moment, Lourana expected to be drained of life or choked by darkness, one or the other.

I can't do it this time, Darrick.

"Brighid?" If she was there, if she was real. "If you can help us . . ."

She saw Rory's hand lift.

Then she was no longer alone.

The room was flooded with a pure light so intense she had to shut her eyes, but even then she could see it.

I am the Bright One.

Lourana felt the light as a pressure around her, but it was the kind of invisible pressure that lifts airplanes into the sky. She was raised up. If the Fomóraigh were the darkest of the earth, the weight of stone on stone, then this was their opposite.

You invoked my help.

The light was clear as noonday sun. She felt it flood into her soul, joy like a shout, joy that saw pain and death and refused their power.

"Brighid?"

I am the Queen of Life, the Strength of Woman. I am the Mourning Mother.

Lourana felt that connection plunge straight through her.

She heard mothers weeping, throughout all time. Demeter weeping as she looked for her daughter, stolen away to the underworld.

She heard Ubbiri crying for Jivanti, her 84,000 daughters burned on the burning-ground.

She heard Brighid herself, mourning her son Ruadan.

That was the first lament raised over Eire.

Lourana heard the mothers of warriors and the mothers of sailors, mothers of children lost to plague, mothers of the famine dead, all keening.

Lourana heard herself, as she had sometimes sung in her cottage, old songs that Dreama loved, that might somehow bring her home. She sang until the notes became wailing, until she had no more voice to give grief. And then at last she had found her lost daughter, in the embrace of the dead.

I lean over every cradle, singing, and over every graveside, weeping.

Lourana could see, now, in the brightness, that a tall woman stood with children on one hand, and on the other, the living assembled around a grave. Life came and life left, and women bore the pangs of both.

It is your weakness and your strength.

Now she was shown a battlefield beside a lake, and on one side the Fomóraigh, a wall of giants led by a giant with one deadly eye, and on the other, Brighid and her kin, most bright and beautiful like her, some divided in their nature, children born of the People of Dana and the Fomóraigh in their long standoff. They lifted their spears and shook them; crows circled in the sky.

Kings and warriors raised the walls of Dún Ailinne, but older still is the endless fire of Cill Dara, sanctuary of the oak trees.

The armies rushed together, and the Bright One, the Victorious, fought beside her dark sisters. Lourana saw her armored and armed, her light become flame, and she advanced on the beings from the sea-depths at The Last Battle of Mag Tuired. Lourana was with Brighid as the Tuatha Dé pushed the Fomóraigh back to the roots of the mountains where humans did not go, into the deepest places of the sea beyond the reach of fishermen's nets.

Lourana raised an ancient battle cry that was also a keen, mourning the dead and the lost even before the battle began. Enclosed in a flame that did not burn, she moved against Rory and the dark.

Chapter 42

Rory endured, despite Padraig, despite the creatures roused from the coal, secreted in the place that had sustained him ever since the legacy passed to him and where the others had not been able to follow.

He thought it was just a matter of time.

His father grew stronger it seemed with every day, augmented by the ancestors and now this alien beast that had infiltrated him body and soul. For the first time, he understood that phrase. Dark threads were being woven through his very self. He almost expected them to be visible, under the skin of hands the others now controlled, veining the legs that did not obey him any longer.

Zombie, he thought again. I am the dead come alive.

We are not dead, and will never die. Padraig. *The Fomóraigh told me, let your son take your life, and you will live forever. I gave Domnall my patriarchal blessing.*

Their opponents had showed themselves to be inadequate, as the Fomóraigh had indicated. Cathbad, lacking his robe and staff and air of self-importance, nonetheless had raised his voice against their assembly and been tossed aside. Darrick, too, made an attempt. Rory watched as he had gathered himself and exerted that killing force against him. The Fomóraigh had merely returned it against Darrick.

Rory didn't think the men were dead. He got the sense that there would be time for the Fomóraigh and his ancestors to take everything they wanted from them, to drain every scrap of being from these men who thought they held power, who clutched after the hems of the fairy-folk.

Lourana called out to him. He truly didn't wish to harm her. She asked Cormac to remember Dreama. Cormac had become lost among the other Kavanaghs since he had expelled him from his enclave.

Rory wished he had managed to step in front of a bus before all this, jumped from the top of the KCL building as a disgraced businessman ought, but the others would never have allowed it to happen. He knew because he had made a couple of feints, just the other day at Howth Head, but froze before ever getting close. He would not be allowed to destroy himself. Now he would be trapped forever within the haunted house of the Kavanaghs, with its own resident monster, for generation after generation.

He felt the growing pressure of his fathers to reach out and take Lourana's life.

Even as his hand lifted, an immense light exploded in the room. He choked on an outcry as his ancestors' shock tumbled through his thoughts. Trepidation shivered through the Fomóraigh, a memory of a long-ago battle and the echoes of voices calling *Brighid, Brighid.*

Lourana, clothed with this radiance, began to move toward him. She seemed almost to be its source. Although the others feared this new apparition, Rory did not. She cast her light around him, around them, like a cloak of sunlit snow.

The Fomóraigh moaned like the sea in the hollows of the cliffs, but did not disappear.

Brighid/Lourana, because they seemed to be one being, went first to where Darrick lay like the dead. She knelt and rested her palm on his forehead. He opened his eyes, breathed in deeply, and he reached for her but she moved away.

The dark coiled and shivered around him. Rory felt its tentacles loosen from his mind and body.

Lourana/Brighid went past, her presence billowing the brilliant cloak she'd draped upon him. She bent to the fallen druid and spoke. His eyes opened and he staggered to his feet, then went to his knees before the ruler of his heart.

The light shifted now, from a white as pure as magnesium flashing at the touch of air to the green of light through leaves, shifting, rising and falling, now a pale shadow, now an opening through which the sun shot an arrow.

For a moment, he sank gratefully into the comfort of tree-shadow, as he had while running in forests from Redbird to Galway. He breathed deeply, tasting the freshness of the air, the scent of upturned earth and meadow-herbs.

The green and gold shadows coalesced into solid forms, trees with shaggy-barked trunks and branches red with fruit, limber willows and ancient, twisted pines. The confines of the room dissolved, and he could see trees massing into forest that seemed to extend forever.

These are the trees despoiled from Eire.

As he heard that female voice, Brighid or Lourana, some of the darkness lifted from his body and mind. Rory flexed his hands just to feel the reality of his own body beginning to return to his control.

The druid was standing now, hands raised, head back as he chanted. "Trees return that built the roofs of English churches."

Lourana/Brighid's light washed across the forest, brightening the leafy tops.

Coal is the grave of trees. Eamon.

All the trees of the world are reborn in fire. Domnall.

The Fomóraigh's sense was clear, without words, images of fire chewing through living forest, fire creeping underground in coal seams. Fire, fire, fire. Ash.

Rory saw darkness begin to creep around the roots of the trees, at first like a shadow, then the trickle of black water. No, like coal turned fluid. The rivulets joined and formed a black pavement under the trees. Then, like the threads he had felt creeping through himself, he saw black strands begin to rise along the paths by which trees pull water up from the deep earth. He could hear Padraig chortling.

Brighid/Lourana rallied her troops. *This is the moment!*

The trees brightened. Cathbad was singing, now, and the wind that rustled the tops gathered its voice, the chorus of birds on a spring dawn, a million birds on a million branches.

For a moment, the black tide paused. Rory felt poised on an infinitely small fulcrum.

Then Darrick was there, moving against the darkness, but he wasn't attacking the Kavanaghs or the Fomóraigh directly. Instead, Rory felt his presence shift from the way he'd previously resisted the bludgeoning emotions that powered the assembly. Like a very thin blade, this new Darrick found his way through that armor to the vulnerable inside.

Rory felt the Fomóraigh pull back and consolidate, but Darrick pursed relentlessly, peeling that presence from Rory's awareness. He gasped at the sudden feeling of lightness, as though he'd been carrying an enormous weight that had been lifted.

The forest was singing in every cell, leaf and branch, beast and bird and insect, the humming unseen life.

He saw the ancient ones pulled into the embrace of the trees and fragment into a black rain that fell and joined the retreating darkness on the ground. A pool emptying, a stream running backward, a trickle. Gone.

Rory felt Eamon and Padraig and the others gathering to fight back. Caught between the irrepressible forces of life outside and the implacable forces of destruction within, he was prepared for the end. He made an attempt to reach Cormac and received the faintest reply. *We'll fight Eamon together.*

Darrick's defensive power had become a key that let him enter the haunted house. Rory could sense him moving in his consciousness, and so could the others. Eamon howled at the arrival of his enemy, not at the gates but inside the walls.

Cormac.

Yes, I'm here.

And so the ghost-ridden mansion was assailed from within and without. Rory felt a surprising strength in his uncle's gentle presence. Darrick opened the way, and the light of Brighid/Lourana came in and scoured every dark hall and found its way into the depths. They seemed to be in Knockaulin House itself, a memory palace of ambition from its many-chimneyed top to the deepest space carved from the coal.

Cormac and Cathbad were chanting together, poetry that Rory did not recognize, but their voices blended.

Domnall was the first to go, fleeing down a corridor to shatter against a marble wall. Then Patrick, his grandfather, a sigh of breath, a spirit released.

Eamon went howling, smashing mirrors and pillars until he reached the great fireplace and turned. A fire exploded behind him, and it seemed like he gathered strength from it. Darrick confronted his enemy again, face to face. Eamon shrank, shriveled before implacable justice, collapsed into dust on the hearthstones.

Padraig, last of the combatants, cursed those arrayed against him, retreating down stairs to the last stronghold, the black room. The green light dimmed, but rose again. Cornered, he escaped by tunneling into the coal to rejoin his ancient allies.

Finally there was only Cormac.

The mansion had dissolved back into forest, sun sparkling through the leaves.

We're still here, Rory thought.

Yes, somehow.

I heard your poetry.

Some of it was Yeats, some of it mine. It's good to leave with those words.

Anguish twisted through Rory. He felt the emptiness of an individual solitary on the earth. He had lost his mother, his grandfather, and finally his father, as painful as that connection had been. He couldn't imagine losing his uncle as well. He remembered Cormac once glancing up from a book as Rory passed, downcast from some slight by his father, and his smile and nod gave him the encouragement to set his shoulders back.

Please, send me away.

I will have no one.

It will be a relief to die, though I will miss Dreama.

Rory felt that longing, now become part of him forever. Or as long as forever is, for an ordinary man.

Dear Rory, you will be whole again. I remember what that was like.

Cormac departed, and the song in the trees rose to welcome him.

Chapter 43

Darrick saw Rory slide to the floor, emptied, and knelt beside him. He still breathed, though the Kavanagh heir did not respond to his name or to Darrick taking his cold hands between his. What's left of him, he wondered, after being so fully inhabited by those ghosts and demons.

He turned to Lourana for help but could barely stand to squint at that brightness.

She was still filled, surrounded, with Brighid's intense light. Her face was transformed with the appearance of a saint in ecstasy. Somehow, through that immanence, she remained Lourana, with her hair pulled back and a sweatshirt and jeans, as he'd first encountered her back in Redbird.

She has been a noble vessel, my anchor in this battle. I honor her valiant spirit.

Darrick wondered what he was, as well, now that the crisis was past.

Strong son of the oak, you have grown into this power. You carry the legacy of the brehon, and can comprehend those who are damaged and ease their distress. The world needs those who sustain order with compassion.

Cathbad was staring avidly into the trees, as the forest thinned and began to disappear. Darrick saw them as well, people bright and various moving away along with the trees, like a distant projection from another world. Crowned kings and queens on horseback but also bards with their harps, druids and healers, smiths carrying gold torcs, gardeners with plants — those dedicated to making and tending the world. They were waiting for Brighid to join them.

We return to our Bright Lands. Seldom are we called upon any longer. We will remember you.

The light was gone. And so were they.

The walls of the room had returned, everything looked as it had, even the painting of the little girl on the wall, even the book flopped open on a chair. No one moved, as though they had been turned into statues, but it was only the shock of the everyday world. Then Cathbad dropped down beside him and took over care of Rory. He nodded toward Lourana and Darrick went to her.

He started to embrace her, but at the last moment, pulled back. How did you go about touching a goddess? She grabbed him and pulled him in tight, and as he felt the solid, comfortable shape of her body, nothing otherworldly about it, he relaxed and they breathed a deep sigh of relief in unison.

"It's over," he said.

"I hope." She glanced toward Rory.

"I think they're all gone," he said. "What do you remember?"

"I remember you and Cathbad, I thought you were dead, and then Brighid was there and she was all around me. Then trees. It was beautiful, but the Fomóraigh were destroying it all, sending poison into the world. You know what that reminded me of."

Darrick nodded. Who could forget the Broad River choked with orange glop?

"I was frightened they were winning, then a great peace came over me. Everything was going to be all right. You were kicking the old Kavanaghs out of Rory somehow, like we were in Knockaulin House and opening every door and window, letting the daylight in and pushing the darkness out."

"I remember some of that."

"I thought you were dead for sure."

"I think I was, or almost. The Fomóraigh turned my own power back on me. The impact stopped my heart, I think, because I felt my spirit letting go of my body." He glanced over at Rory, who hadn't moved. "Then I saw her, or you, and I was called back from the depths."

"Me?"

"A woman opened her arms to accept me. I thought it was you, then I thought it was Brighid, then Mary. Maybe it was all three."

Lourana hummed a couple of bars of "Let It Be," and gave him that crooked smile. He thought he could still see a brightness about her, but her eyes were again her own.

Chapter 44

Rory woke up staring at a white ceiling, plaster applied in swirls, crossed by a jagged crack from side to side. It wasn't Knockaulin House, though he remembered being there somehow. For a moment, he lay quiet and tried to figure out where he was and what had happened.

He turned his head to see Darrick, Cathbad, and Lourana watching him. They sat somberly in a row and looked like a panel of judges at a skating competition. He almost expected them to lift up scorecards.

"I'm still in Kildare?"

Lourana nodded.

"Can I get up?"

"If you feel able," said Cathbad.

He sat up, swung his feet off the bed, and felt like he might just tip over, or fly away. The solidity that had settled in him with his ancestors was gone. After a moment, he stood and walked to a chair in the corner, and was happy to sit back down. They watched him closely.

They wonder what I am now. If I'm still a Kavanagh, like the Kavanaghs used to be. He listened for the voices that used to fill his head, but there was no sound. Not a rumble or a sneer or the commentary of Cormac. No voices. And no hunger.

"How do you feel?" asked Darrick.

"Like everything, everyone, is gone."

"We cleaned house," Darrick said.

Lourana looked at him intently. "We think we did, anyway. How can we be sure?"

Her eyes were very bright, as though something had stayed with her after Brighid had gone, insinuated now into her being the way the Fomóraigh had laced itself through him. He wondered if every trace of that possession was gone. He felt like an exotic deep-sea specimen just dragged aboard a research vessel.

"If you're not sure, will you kill me?" Rory looked at Darrick, who must still have his powers. He could sense the difference in him, a new authority. Nothing preternatural would be needed to kill me now, Rory knew. Any common knife or bullet would do.

"That's not what we mean," Darrick said gently.

If he should die, it wouldn't be unexpected. He and Cormac had always thought it would end up that way. He had been on that roller-coaster — fatalistic, hopeful, despairing, hopeful again.

"But we would have to try again to free you."

"So what do I do to prove it?"

"I want you to test yourself against me."

Rory closed his eyes and tried to find that pulsing hunger that drove him for a time, the one he hadn't known until his inheritance from Eamon. He searched and found nothing, not even that light touch his grandfather had taught him.

"May I touch you?"

Darrick nodded.

He walked over to Darrick, who stood to meet him. He tried the gentle tug he had been taught first, to start a brief shimmer of life moving from someone else into him. The gift inborn. The sharing, as he'd been taught. Was that, too, part of the Fomóraigh legacy? He touched Darrick's shoulder and waited for the light to begin, for the sense of renewed energy and strength. Then he put both hands on his shoulders and willed the transfer to happen.

Nothing. That legacy had gone away with the ancient creatures, back to where it came from. He remembered his face pressed against the damp rock in the Irish mine, the movement of the Fomóraigh within the coal. But that moment was just a memory, already fading.

"Could you sense anything?" He remembered the moment Darrick entered his mind, the shock of a presence that wasn't linked by blood.

"Nothing." Darrick smiled. "It appears you are just an ordinary man."

Cathbad also gave his approval. "I don't feel anything untoward in Rory. He's been liberated."

Liberated. Rory thought that was probably the right word, but he felt emptied as well. Free but abandoned, like a city where the troops have entered and then harried the invaders away, leaving the streets silent.

"I scarcely know myself now, without the others. Especially Cormac." Rory struggled against the break in his voice. "It was hard to let him go."

He waited for a whisper, a sense, but nothing. All that remained of Cormac was a new and sensual appreciation of the world.

"I remember that you are an orphan," he said, turning to Darrick.

"Now you are as well. But you were Rory before all this and will be Rory again," he replied.

Rory thought about the surcease of running. He thought about school, books, spreadsheets, the career set out before him. Money. Money and power. Nothing that he cared about any longer.

"Can I ask . . ."

He glanced toward Lourana.

"What?"

"I'd like to speak with Dreama. She needs to know."

Lourana handed over her phone, without looking at Darrick.

Rory retreated behind a closed door. He saw that she had called several times, in those disordered hours, and sent texts and messages on every platform. After the encounter in the coal mine and the anger that had led him to eject Cormac, he'd not bothered to check. He'd had no concern for her or anyone else.

"Hi. Rory?" Her face filled the screen and her hair was tangled.

"Hi, Dreama."

"Where have you been? I've been worried sick, not hearing anything."

"They're gone, Dreama."

"Who?"

"My father and grandfather, all of them, all the Kavanaghs."

"How?"

"Darrick and your mother, and — others."

"And Cormac?"

"I'm sorry. He's gone too."

He could see, even on the small screen, the tears beginning to roll down her cheeks. "Are you sure?"

"Yes, he's gone." He felt that emptiness echo with his words. "I miss him."

"I don't understand."

"Eamon, well, I guess me, chased Darrick and Lourana to Ireland and all up and down, trying to kill them. Finally Darrick was able to force them out of my mind. But Cormac helped. He wanted an end. Neither one of us could stand being bound together with my father and the rest forever."

Dreama turned away and he heard her snuffle, blow her nose, and come back red-faced and sad.

"I'm an ordinary guy now. Just Rory."

"It's all too much, isn't it? With the company and all?"

"What about the company?"

"You don't know?"

"I've been out of touch."

"It's bad news. The TV said it imploded. Financial ruin. And a lot more, investigations. I didn't catch all of it."

Rory stared out the window at the green countryside. Someone was flying a kite. He could see the red shape of it dipping and swirling.

"I guess I'm a poor man now, Dreama. It's actually a relief. I couldn't go back to KCL. I don't care at all about that world. I don't want to think about coal again, ever in my life."

"You still have your home."

"Not a home. A house, that terrible house." It rose up in his memory, its hundreds of glittering window panes, its chilly rooms and chamber of secrets. "What to do with that?"

"I guess it can be sold."

"Or maybe I can give it to a charity and hope some kindhearted people will be able to cleanse it."

A long silence developed.

"I'm not Cormac any more," he began. "But I know that, being together as we were, he left me with some things. Opened my eyes. I can begin to see the world now the way he taught me, through the senses, through poetry."

She gave a little cough, a stifled sob.

"I would like to remain in your life."

"I don't know. It's not the way we planned, is it?"

He knew she was still talking to Cormac. "It's no fairy tale, Dreama. I don't know who I am now, at so many levels. And maybe you need some time to finish grieving Cormac. But then, I would, I would like to see you."

Chapter 45

"I'm not leaving til we go."

"It's just a tourist trap." Darrick had looked up from where he was rolling his polo shirts into neat, wrinkle-free packets.

"Maybe, but I can't go back to West Virginia and tell people I was in Ireland and didn't kiss the Blarney Stone."

And so they'd detoured southeast to the gray tower weather-streaked with black. Another band of rain blew through and made everything shine like a picture postcard, all the square fields bounded with hedges. At the Castle, they'd waited in line until she found herself climbing the stone stairs, all 128 of them, to the top of the tower to kiss the stone and gain the gift of gab. Alone.

"I've had enough of the supernatural to last me for a while," Darrick had said. Secretly, she was pretty sure that he was afraid of heights.

Spiral stairs brought her to the top, to a stone walkway that paced the four sides of the tower, with crenellations to let bowmen shoot down from the top and pour boiling oil, she guessed, on the attackers. The tower looked down on two smaller round towers, a stream, and gardens in bloom.

Ahead, she saw people lying on their backs to reach the stone, which seemed pretty awkward, but there was just the one special stone and it was on the outside. It seemed like whichever origin story was true, the grateful witch or the druid's daughter, that they could have chosen to put the rock on the inside somewhere.

A man cleaned the surface with a spray bottle and cloth — germs weren't prevented by the spell — and explained the process of lying down on your back, grabbing hold of two black bars, and leaning back.

"Keep looking up at the sky, not down to the ground," he advised.

He held her around the waist as she dipped her head. Her ponytail went flying loose as she put her lips to the smooth place where a million others, famous people and average folks, had placed theirs.

And it was over, she came back up and got to her feet, receiving a ticket to collect her photo downstairs. "So you'll not forget our Emerald Isle!"

Not much chance of that.

Darrick wasn't impressed when he saw the picture. "I can't tell it's you," he said.

They walked for a little while in the gardens, saw the standing stones and the druids' cave. It reminded her of Cathbad, and must have reminded Darrick as well, because neither one of them was talking much.

They'd said goodbye to the druid on the outskirts of Kildare. Lourana thought how strange it was, that she now considered him "the druid" without any sarcasm.

He'd charged Darrick to use his powers as "a force for good in the world" and reminded him that his role was not law-giver nor vigilante, but to protect and maintain the boundaries and mediate disputes.

He'd embraced Lourana and given her a kiss on the cheek.

"You're just beginning your journey, my dear. I knew that well before the battle, when you began sending your thoughts out. No, I could not read your mind from the outside. Like Darrick, I received your words."

She was taken aback at that. What Darrick heard, how the druid had responded to her thoughts — all her doing.

"My mother had second sight, and her mother before. I never could see the future."

"Maybe not see it, but change it," Cathbad said.

"What about you?" Darrick asked.

"Oh, I'll continue as I have, teaching the young and entertaining the tourists." Cathbad's banter fell a little flat, to her ear.

"Did Brighid leave you with any message?" she asked.

"More than a message. I've called upon Brighid many, many times for our ceremonies, and could raise the lesser light, but I've never been challenged to do anything mighty. Never asked of her, never challenged myself, truth be told. Now that I've encountered her, bright in glory and strength, I can't go back to pushing small potatoes around my plate. Time for Cathbad to be working."

"You've done a mighty work with the Kavanaghs," Darrick said.

"Thank you. We all did. A rip in the world has been mended, the Fomoráigh dispatched back to their depths, and the living pulled from the embrace of the dead."

"That's a clear win, in my book," Lourana said. Cathbad met her encouraging gaze but seemed if anything more somber.

"The world is changing, as it has always, but too rapidly. Have you not seen it in your home place, the storms out of season?"

She nodded.

"Everything is ruled by the clock of the heavens, the seasons cycling, and we've knocked it off kilter, you, me, all of us, with our smokes and engines. We're all guilty, all liable to the penalties. Yet there's hope. We do as we must — plant trees proper to the land, scatter seed, preserve and protect and make small gains. Each of us guilty, each of us bound to act."

It was like they were the Three Musketeers or something, parting to go in different directions. Lourana reflected on his charge as they made their way from Blarney Castle and turned toward Dublin.

"Is there anything else you wanted to see?" Darrick asked, breaking her silence.

"Not really. It's pretty and all, but I'm ready to go home."

"Did the Blarney Stone give you the gift of eloquence?"

She gave him a smile. "I sure hope so. I need to be able to come up with plausible lies for where we've been all this time."

"Then maybe I should have kissed the stone too."

She thought about what waited for them back in West Virginia. A new start seemed possible. The Kavanaghs weren't a problem any more, and whatever might happen with Dreama was out of her control. She'd fessed up to Darrick, who had forgiven her secrecy about Rory and her daughter. Darrick had his job to go back to, though he'd been saying things that made her think he would not be content with the routine of an auditor any longer. She didn't yet know what her purpose might be. The struggle to save her daughter and bring down the Kavanaghs, that was finished. But the rivers were still poisoned and the mountaintops being dumped in the valleys. She might have something to say about that.

Meanwhile, she had one other thing that had to be done. She just didn't know how to go about it.

They dropped off the little car, which had served them well. Seemed like she'd spent more time on the road than anywhere else, running from one side of the country to the other, though Killeshandra would always be dear to her. That forest with the fairy doors at the foot of the trees. She wondered if that was an old forest, if Cathbad and his grove knew about it or maybe went there.

The concourse was busy, people hustling to the gates or waiting for an arrival.

"Do we need to find the chapel?" she asked.

"Because I've turned religious now? Not really. I've had my eyes — opened. But I'm not sure what it is I've seen."

"No, silly, to get away from people."

"Not any more. I can still feel their emotions, but it's manageable. It doesn't make me try to hide or shove the pain away. Maybe I'll be able to do something with this gift, if it is one. I don't know."

"For sure we'll never be the same." Lourana sat down and settled her luggage around her. "We thought it was done after the black room and Marco and all, but this time it feels like it really is over and done with."

"Do you want a coffee?" Darrick pointed out a Starbucks across the concourse.

"Sure."

He was a long time getting it, so Lourana had time to think. Time to figure out what she could say, or should say.

When he came with the cups, he stood looking at her as though he had something on his mind as well. "Do you feel like Brighid is . . ."

"Still here?"

He nodded.

"I remember that sense of peace but also strength, like while she was with me I could have done just about anything as long as it was intended for good. But it's just a memory now. Rory said something of Cormac has stayed with him, but he's not *there* any more."

"One thing I'd hoped for, I guess, but it didn't happen. I wasn't healed." Darrick's voice was shadowed with regret. "I guess that was too much to hope for, that because of Brighid's touch the ataxia would be gone."

Lourana felt like that was her opening. "You asked if Brighid was still with me, and I told you it was all pretty hazy while she was running the show. But as she was leaving, she let me see something."

He cocked his head.

"I don't think it's an answer, but maybe the start of one. She showed me your parents."

He leaned close.

"They couldn't marry, your parents. They were both in the church, a nun and I don't know how to explain the man except he was some kind of priest. High up in the church. They loved each other but they loved the church just as much."

"Like Abelard and Heloise."

She nodded, though she didn't know much about that.

"Brighid wanted you to know that you came from love and you were loved, even if briefly. The man, your father, knew his brehon legacy and gave you a fitting name. They made sure you would be taken care of."

She sensed that he was disappointed, that this was a sort of inadequate answer. There was more that Brighid told her, but she made it clear that it was women's business and not to be shared except with Dreama.

Their flight was announced and from there it was all about boarding and settling in. Then they were taxiing and lifting off through clouds that suddenly broke. She saw farmlands passing under them, the fields and the little hills, then some long lakes, the glint of rivers. She wondered if that might be County Cavan, all that water. Suddenly, she was homesick for this place. It had become as much a part of her as West Virginia's green rolling hills.

Lourana turned from the window. She put her hand on Darrick's, got his attention from whatever deep place he was visiting.

"Let's try this again."

She took off the claddagh ring, and he turned it around so that it pointed to her heart.

Acknowledgments

Boundless thanks to the Weymouth Center for the Arts and Humanities for a retreat week in which I made dramatic progress on this story, the North Carolina Department of Cultural and Natural Resources regional artist grant program for its support, Sarah Lindsay for her sharp editor's eye, and my all-star writing "squad" of Grace Marcus, Kevin Rippin, T. Frohock, and Al Sirois, for close reads and wise comments.